D0648113

BILL PENNANT, BABE RUTH, AND ME

BILL PENNANT, BABE RUTH, AND ME

TIMOTHY TOCHER

Cricket Books
Chicago

Text © 2009 by Timothy Tocher
All rights reserved
Printed in the United States of America
Designed by Ann Dillon
First edition, 2009

Special thanks to my editor, Deborah Vetter. Debby immerses herself in a manuscript until she knows the material better than the writer. Her ear for language and attention to detail are invaluable.

—T.T.

Library of Congress Cataloging-in-Publication Data

Tocher, Timothy.
    Bill Pennant, Babe Ruth, and me / Timothy Tocher.—1st ed.
        p. cm.
    Summary: In 1920, sixteen-year-old Hank finds his loyalties divided when he is assigned to care for the Giants' mascot, a wildcat named Bill Pennant, as well as keep an eye on Babe Ruth in Ruth's first season with the New York Yankees.
    ISBN-13: 978-0-8126-2755-8
    ISBN-10: 0-8126-2755-5
    [1. Baseball—Fiction. 2. Wildcat—Fiction. 3. Sports team mascots—Fiction. 4. Ruth, Babe, 1895–1948—Fiction. 5. New York Giants (Baseball team)—Fiction. 6. New York Yankees (Baseball team)—Fiction. 7. McGraw, John Joseph, 1873–1934—Fiction. 8. New York (State)—History—20th century—Fiction.] I. Title.
    PZ7.T5637Bil 2009
    [Fic]—dc22

                                                        2008026829

For Judy

The Newest Giant

I t's no fun being sent for by the headmaster. Trudging through the slushy snow, I wondered why old Jebediah Adams wanted to see me. I must have done something one of the teachers here at Anson Academy didn't like. Not that I'm wild. It's just that this place has more rules than checkers.

My foot slipped, and icy slush found its way inside my shoe. Here I was freezing in New York when I should be at spring training in San Antonio, Texas, with John McGraw and the Giants. I had been a good-luck charm and all-around helper to the famous manager during the 1919 season and expected to be the same this year. Instead, McGraw and his wife had stuck me in this fancy boarding school outside New York City.

I climbed the steps to Branley Hall and rapped on the

headmaster's door. "Come in," he called in his creaky voice. A blast of heat met me. Jebediah Adams had his desk so close to the blazing fireplace that reflected flames danced on its polished surface. Sweat ran down my brow, so I yanked off my hat.

"Well done, Cobb. You've remembered your manners," the headmaster croaked. Everyone at Anson Academy was called by their last name, even if it was one you had chosen for yourself. I had borrowed mine from Ty Cobb, the greatest living ballplayer.

"How are you progressing with your studies?" the headmaster asked.

When I first came to Anson Academy, I was lost. I thought Ancient Greece was the stuff the cook used to fry potatoes. Now, most of the time, I understand what the teachers are talking about, so I said, "I'm doing good, sir."

Adams winced. "Even your grammar. Are you doing *well* with that, Cobb?"

I'd just told him how good I was doing. Maybe he was losing his hearing. I nodded my head.

He sighed. "Spring recess begins on Friday. I've received a telegram from Mr. McGraw asking if we can spare you before then. What do you say, Cobb; are you interested in missing school this week and going to San Antonio?"

A jolt of excitement shot through me. I didn't own up to it, but I planned on leaving and never coming back. I was going to be a baseballer. Everything I needed to know I could learn on the diamond. I'd given school a try to please the McGraws, but it wasn't for me. Growing up wandering the country with my old man had spoiled me for staying in one place. But I was curious, too. I knew McGraw wouldn't send for me unless he had a reason. "Do you know why I'm wanted, sir?"

The headmaster rooted through some papers on his desk, found the Western Union form, and held it close to his watery eyes. "Please send Hank Cobb first available train. Will take charge of newest Giant Bill Pennant."

Who was Bill Pennant, and how could I take charge of a ballplayer? It didn't matter as long as it put me with the team. "When can I leave, sir?"

Mr. Adams winced again. His rheumatism might have been acting up. "You *may* leave in twenty minutes. Our jitney will drive you to the train station."

That gave me time to slog back to the empty dormitory. I stuffed my mitt in my shirt and pocketed the few dollars I kept hidden in the toe of a fancy pair of shoes McGraw had given me. I rolled up some underwear and socks inside a clean shirt and used the sleeves to tie the package. When the jitney pulled up, I was standing on the steps waiting.

The sloppy roads slowed us down. I had just enough time to buy a copy of the Spalding Guide from a newsstand before climbing on board a train bound for points south. During the two days and several trains it took me to reach Texas, I nearly wore the print off the pages. It was crammed with statistics from the past season. But what really interested me were the articles on the season that lay ahead.

A chart showed the players teams had gained and lost

in trades since last season. Most of the attention was on the Yankees, an American League team previously ignored by the sportswriters and people of New York. The Yankees didn't even have their own stadium, instead renting the Polo Grounds when the Giants were on the road. I had never seen them play and hadn't thought I was missing much, either.

But this year would be different. Back in January, the Yankees had paid more money than I could imagine—$125,000—to buy Babe Ruth from the Boston Red Sox. Suddenly folks were talking about the Yankees, too.

All Babe had done was help the Red Sox win the World Series in 1916 and 1918 with his great pitching. Then last year, he had played the outfield full time. I still couldn't believe it, but Babe had hit twenty-nine home runs, more than anyone else in the history of baseball.

As happy as the Yankee bugs were, that's how mad the Red Sox fanatics found themselves. Why would a team get rid of a player who was young, healthy, and had already set records as a pitcher and a hitter? I couldn't wait to get to spring training to see what John McGraw thought about the deal.

Not that McGraw had been talkative lately. When I'd visited him over the Christmas holidays, he'd spent hours at his desk, staring into space. I told myself that he was plotting to get the Giants back to the World Series. But there had to be something eating him. McGraw used to like to talk baseball with me. Now he hardly bothered.

While I was finding out how dumb I was at Anson Academy, he had been to the World Series in Cincinnati and Chicago. I thought he'd be tickled pink that the

National League Reds had won, especially since the experts had picked the White Sox. But he got an odd look on his face every time I brought up the topic. I didn't know any more about the games than what I had read in the papers.

On my journey, I read every sports page I could get my hands on. There were plenty of stories on the Giants, but never a mention of Bill Pennant. Leave it to McGraw to come up with a new player and keep it secret.

I hoped Bill Pennant was a pitcher. The Giants had been short-handed in that department last year, and with my best friend, Chief Sunrise, gone off to pitch in the Negro National League, they figured to be wanting again.

The best part of the trip was that the farther I went, the more it looked like spring. We chugged past the last dirty snowbanks in Maryland, coated blooming flowers with our ash in Virginia, and blew smoke at ballplayers practicing in fields near the tracks in the Carolinas. By the time we reached Texas, I had forgotten all about winter.

I got off at the San Antonio train station and tried to adjust to being on foot. My heart beat time like a steam engine after that long ride. I asked a man selling news-papers on the platform for directions to Bears Stadium and set off down South Presa Street, the sun loosening the tight muscles in my back and legs as I walked.

Enjoying the fine weather, I ambled along until I was within a block of the ballpark. Then my ears picked up the sounds that stirred my soul: the crack of bat on ball, the slap of ball on leather, and the buzz of reaction from a crowd.

I was almost running by the time I slipped through

the unguarded gate and burst into the stands for my first look at the 1920 edition of the New York Giants. I was too far away to see faces, but I could pick out players by quirks I had come to know last season.

George Burns raced across the outfield, his baseball cap sporting an extra-long bill that gave him the look of a kid wearing his father's hat. Folks made fun of that cap, but George had never been known to lose a fly ball in the sun. Pep Youngs tapped his glove against his leg as he manned right field. I knew Oil Smith was crouched behind the plate from his habit of lifting his mask to spit each time he threw the ball to the pitcher.

The man I most wanted to see, John McGraw, was right where I expected to find him, in the middle of the action. A player I didn't recognize was out near second base, and McGraw was peppering him with slashing grounders and sassy remarks.

"Get your butt down when you field a ball. I can read the scoreboard through your legs," was one choice comment. The rookie let a ball scoot past him and kicked the ground in disgust. "Dip your mitt in that dirt instead of your cleats and you might catch the ball." With that McGraw slammed one right at him. The ball rolled up the rookie's arm, over his shoulder, and into the outfield.

This had to be Bill Pennant. My chest swelled with pride. Slick fielding was my specialty. I'll bet McGraw brought me down here to show this guy how to play his position. He hit another grounder. The rookie fielded it cleanly, but threw the ball into the seats behind first base. Shaking his head, McGraw walked toward the dugout.

The Newest Giant

I stepped over the low railing that separated the stands from the field of play to meet him. John McGraw was near the third baseline when he spotted me. A smile replaced the sour look those misplayed grounders had pasted on his face.

"Hank! You made it," he said.

I did a double take when I saw his uniform. McGraw was usually the nattiest man in the ballpark, yet the jersey he wore was in tatters. It looked as if someone had sharpened a knife on it.

McGraw grabbed my outstretched hand. His grip was as firm as ever. You had to be ready or he would crush your knuckles. But something was different. McGraw sensed it, too, narrowing his eyes to stare at me. "Wasn't I taller than you last season?"

My jaw dropped. I was finally growing. McGraw was only five feet seven, but he had towered over me last April. It just shows what eating regular can do for a fellow. The food at Anson Academy wouldn't win any contests, but there was a lot of it, and I never failed to take my share.

"Size will help," McGraw said. "You can't let Bill Pennant think you're scared of him."

I pointed at the rookie, who seemed to be trying to hide inside his baggy uniform. "Why would I be scared of him? He's just another ballplayer."

McGraw's brow furrowed. Then he saw where I was pointing. "That's not Bill Pennant," he said with a laugh. "You think I need help whipping a rookie into shape? Bill's in the locker room. Walk through to the back and open the last door on the right. I want you two to get to know each other. You're going to spend a lot of time together this season."

That sounded good to me. There was no mention of my going back to school. But I was confused, too. Why wasn't Bill Pennant out here on the field with everyone else? I thought he might be injured and need someone to help him work back into shape.

The locker room was quiet. There was the usual mess of players' belongings on the benches, and you could smell the mildew growing in the cold-water showers. I felt strange hunting up a fellow I had never met, but if that was what it took to be part of the team, that was what I would do.

Rapping the door with my knuckles, I called, "Bill Pennant, you in there?" The only answer was a thump, as if something had been thrown at the door. Blood rushed to my face. I wasn't about to take that kind of treatment from anyone. If McGraw wanted me to work with Bill Pennant, I was going to work with him.

I turned the knob and yanked open the door only to be met by a blur of fur and claws and a snarl of fury. I was flat on my back on the locker room floor while some sort of creature buried its claws in me. A paw flashed, and I felt the sting of blood on my face. No wonder Bill Pennant hadn't answered. This beast had probably killed him.

My free hand found one of the thick, woolen sweaters the players sometimes wore. I threw it over the critter. With a lot of hissing and spitting, the wildcat—for I saw now that's what it was—abandoned me and commenced to turning the sweater into tufts of wool.

I crawled backward until I whacked my head on one of the benches. Then I used the bench to pull myself to my feet. I stood, legs wobbly, and watched as the wildcat sank its fangs into the sweater, swinging it in its jaws like a captured rabbit. Suddenly, it slung the sweater to the floor, lay down on top of it, and gave a comically huge yawn.

Laughter behind me snapped my head around. John McGraw and Smoky, the team's trainer and equipment manager, rocked on their heels, tears streaming down their faces. At last McGraw got enough control to ask, "How do you like your new roommate?"

Game Plan

moky stopped laughing when he saw the scratches on my cheek. John McGraw's right-hand man, Smoky took care of gear and uniforms, bandaged cuts and bruises, massaged sore muscles, and kept an eye out for players who missed curfew. His hair was the same shade of gray as the Giants' road uniforms, and his black skin had a silvery tinge to it, like the outside of a piece of charcoal that's been burning for a while. He moved slowly, but never wasted a motion. When you shared a job, you felt like you worked twice as hard, but got half as much done. Smoky fetched a basin of water and washed my wounds, then stung me half to death with some iodine.

John McGraw sat on the floor, rubbing Bill Pennant's belly. The cat rumbled like a motorcycle engine, his claws further unraveling McGraw's jersey. Even Bill Pennant's purring sounded dangerous.

"Where'd you get him?" I asked.

"Buddies of mine were hunting in Mexico. They shot his mother, then found him. They didn't have the heart to leave him to starve, so they brought him back. He's going to bring us a lot of luck this year."

John McGraw was a brilliant manager, but it would be hard to find a more superstitious person. He thought crossed bats were a jinx. A bat boy could lose his job for letting handles overlap. If one of the Giants stepped on a chalk line, he would be blamed for any disaster that followed. When I first met McGraw, I'd had a run-in with some cooties. He became convinced that my bald head was lucky and kept me around just to rub my skull at crucial parts of a ball game.

Smoky frowned. I'll bet he was thinking of the torn uniforms and puncture wounds he would be expected to repair. McGraw got to his feet, throwing Bill Pennant an old baseball as he left. The cat let it roll toward the wall, then pounced and began chewing the stitches.

Bill Pennant was no taller than a house cat, but had a much thicker chest. His yellowish brown coat was spotted, like that of a leopard I'd seen in a book at Anson Academy. It looked as if his ears were pointy, but if you got close, you'd see that a tuft of wiry hair stuck up from the top of each one.

More than anything, you noticed his paws, and I'm not just saying that because of the beating he'd given me. They were round and way too big for his body. It looked like he was walking on snowshoes. I slumped on a bench and scratched my head. How was I going to control this animal?

Smoky read my mind. "I'll show you what we've worked out so far, Hank." He led me through the door I had opened to get my first look at Bill Pennant. The room, actually a closet, had shelves from floor to ceiling. The shelves were bare except for a chewed-up sock, the scraps of what used to be a Giants cap, and a bloody clump of feathers.

I raised my eyebrows and pointed. "Pigeon landed on the dugout steps yesterday," Smoky said. "Don't touch what's left. Bill's not done with it, and he reacts badly."

My shoulders sagged another inch. Smoky picked up a metal bowl from the floor. "Bang this dish and Bill will come flying in here to eat. Duck out and slam the door. That's how we lock him up for the night."

"Where do I get the food?"

Smoky reached into his pocket and pulled out a small metal can with a key stuck to its bottom. "I bought a case of these here sardines. There's more in my desk. Bill's been eating them for a week, and we haven't had a complaint yet."

"Does he really stay in the ballpark by himself at night?" I asked. I almost felt sorry for the cat, even though he'd tried to slice me to pieces.

"Not anymore," Smoky said. "Now he's got you."

My mouth was still hanging open when the players trooped in from the diamond. Smoky kicked Bill's baseball. It rolled into the closet. When Bill Pennant chased after it, Smoky closed the door.

"Look who's here," Art Fletcher, the veteran shortstop, greeted me. This took me by surprise, since last year he hadn't spoken to me. "You keep growing, we might make a ballplayer of you yet."

Pep Youngs said, "Hank," as if we'd seen each other yesterday. Jesse Barnes, the team's ace pitcher, nodded and smiled. Oil Smith spat a stream of tobacco juice at my shoes. When I jumped aside in time to avoid the stains, he said, "Good reflexes."

All this attention was confusing me. Smoky put an arm on my shoulder and said, "You're not a rookie anymore, Hank. The boys are used to having you around."

Most of the players filed out in their filthy uniforms, as if they would rather bathe at the hotel where there was at least the possibility of hot water. I knew from experience that some of them wouldn't wash at all. While I helped Smoky straighten up the place, I asked, "Where do I sleep?"

He led me into his office, the room next to Bill Pennant's. Against one wall was an army cot covered by a blanket that looked like it had been put to heavy use in the Great War. "It's not so bad, Hank. I know you're used to living rough."

"Why can't I stay with the team?"

"Bill Pennant did so much damage at the Menger Hotel that the owners threatened to kick us out. We got permission to keep him in the ballpark, but only as long as he behaves himself. I been sleeping here for three nights, making sure he don't get into mischief. Now it's your turn."

"But what will I do here by myself?"

"Train him."

"You're not serious."

"John McGraw's serious. He wants you working with Bill after practice. By opening day he expects that cat to be tame enough for you to lead him around the field."

That seemed impossible. But I was excited. If I was the only one Bill Pennant would listen to, McGraw would have to keep me with the team. "What do I have to teach him, besides not to kill us in our sleep?"

Smoky slid open a drawer of his desk. He pulled out a leather collar with the letters NY and Bill Pennant's name written in fancy script. He reached in again and came out with a leash.

"Do cats walk on leashes?" I asked.

"This one better, or you can explain it to Mr. McGraw."

After Smoky left, I opened a can of sardines, slopping oil on my pants as I did. I pulled open the closet door, slid in the sardines, and banged it shut again. Seconds later, I heard the can bang off the wall as if Bill had batted it with one of his oversized paws.

I needed some fresh air, so I sat on the top step of the dugout and wasted a few minutes feeling sorry for myself. Then I realized that things could be a lot worse. I was in a ballpark, not a dormitory.

The sun cast long shadows on the outfield grass. The beat-up wooden stands sagged toward the playing field from all the years the bugs had leaned into the action.

I couldn't help myself. I grabbed a bat from the rack and took my stance in the batter's box, imagining I was facing Burleigh Grimes, the spitballing star of the Robins.

Grimes tossed a couple of his finest, the spray splattering my face as the pitches dipped and slid away from the plate. I let them go by, crouched, and waited for his fast one.

Grimes threw it over the plate, and I took this little, inside-out swing I'd been working on in the dormitory at night. The first baseman was playing shallow to guard against a bunt, and I blooped the ball over his head. It landed fair, then spun across the foul line, rolling away from the right fielder as I tore down the baseline. I rounded first and dug for second, the roar of the imaginary crowd ringing in my ears. My longer legs needed fewer strides to take me from base to base than they had last season. I felt like I was flying through the Texas twilight.

I cut the bag at second, never thinking of stopping. In my mind, McGraw was coaching third. When I looked his way, he pressed both palms toward the ground—the signal to slide. I watched the third baseman dip to the home plate side of the bag to take the right fielder's throw. I threw myself at him, legs cutting toward the bag. In my fantasy, the baseball ticked off my arm and rolled into foul territory. I scrambled to my feet and headed for home, sliding around the catcher, and slapping the plate with my hand as I skidded past. Dusting myself off, I trotted to the dugout as the bugs shook the ballpark with their cheers.

Lion
Tamer

T he thump of Bill Pennant throwing himself
against the closet door woke me. I went to
Smoky's desk for a can of sardines and pocketed
the collar and leash. Maybe, once Bill Pennant had eaten,
he would be calm enough to stand some training.

I cracked the door, and Bill shot out before I could
stop him. He sprinted for the diamond with me close
behind. I stopped when he squatted in the on-deck circle.
Having done his business, he scratched the loose dirt with
his paws to bury the evidence. Then he walked toward
me. I was tempted to run, but stood my ground.

Bill circled me once, then began rubbing his head
against my pants legs, sounding that menacing purr of his.
I took a slow step onto the grass, and Bill followed. There
was no one else in the ballpark, so I decided to take a
chance. I walked to home plate. Bill joined me.

I started toward first base. Bill passed between my legs. I kept going, a grin on my face. Maybe training this cat wasn't going to be so hard after all. I took the turn at first and walked on, Bill following as eager as a puppy.

When I reached second, I sat down on the bag, Bill Pennant nuzzling my pants cuffs. Ever so slowly, I pulled his collar from my pocket. I scratched Bill's head, and he leaned in, not seeming to mind at all. "You're not so tough, are you?" I cooed. Sinking my fingers into the thick fur on the back of his neck, I held Bill with one hand and tried to slip the collar around his neck with the other.

Before I could blink, Bill batted the collar from my hands. He speared that leather strap with his claws and wrestled it as if it were a snake. I was afraid to touch him again. When he abandoned the collar, I got up and walked to the dugout. To my relief, Bill followed. Only when he was locked in the closet, a bowl of sardines absorbing his attention, did I retrieve that battered collar from the infield.

I would probably have spent the morning trying to figure out why Bill Pennant would follow me like a house pet one minute and fly into a frenzy the next, if Smoky hadn't shown up.

"Morning, Hank. How did you and your roomie sleep?"

"Pretty good. I fed him, so he's probably taking a nap."

"There's a diner just past the Menger Hotel on Alamo Plaza. Go have breakfast, and put it on the team's account. Meanwhile, I'll hunt up a uniform that will fit you now that you're a beanpole."

I realized how hungry I was, and how eager to get back in uniform. I started for the dugout steps at a trot, turning just long enough to ask, "Who we playing today?"

"Yankees. This old park will be rocking with folks wanting to see Babe Ruth."

That put even more spring in my step. As I walked, I massaged my throwing arm, helping it to soak up the San Antonio sunshine. I saw the sign for Alamo Plaza and joined a stream of people turning down the street. The diner must be good to attract this many folks.

San Antonio is kind of a strange town. There were some beautiful buildings, painted up and surrounded by flowers. Then, in the middle of the block, a windowless church had been left to molder. The whole shebang was surrounded by a wall made from the same stone as the church with gaps where gates or doors used to be. Most of the people stopped to gawk, but I kept moving. The idea of breakfast had my stomach doing flips.

I passed the team's hotel. The Menger was gussied up with a fountain and willowy shrubs that would never live through a New York winter. A man was standing out front, waving pennants that said, "Remember the Alamo." Maybe he was trying to organize people to clean up the mess, I don't know.

The diner was diagonally across the street from the hotel. It was doing a bang-up business even though there didn't seem to be a baseballer in sight. The counter had about twenty stools, and all but two were filled by men in white shirts, neckties, and baggy pants. Only their hats showed variety. Some wore winter fedoras while others had switched to the summertime straw hats that matched the San Antonio weather, if not the page on the calendar. One character had on a little round hat. I think it's called a porkpie. I squeezed in next to him, earning a "What'll it be, son?" from the counterman who walked up and down refilling coffee cups.

"Double order of scrambled, grits, bacon, and coffee," I answered and pulled out my Spalding Guide to pass the time.

"Looks like you're a bug," the man in the porkpie said. "Going to the game today?"

"I'm with the Giants," I answered, sticking out my hand. "Name's Hank."

"Damon," he offered as we shook. "When you say you're with the Giants, does that mean you root for them, or do you have a professional affiliation?"

"The second one, if it means that I work for the team." He nodded, so I went on. "Last year I was good-luck charm and bat boy. This season I'm lion tamer."

Damon laughed. "I'll admit it. I never knew of a ball club that carried a lion tamer."

"The Giants may be the first," I said, clearing my elbows off the counter to make room for my eggs.

"How many lions does McGraw have?" The stranger smiled and passed me the salt and pepper.

"Just the one, a Mexican wildcat named Bill Pennant."

Damon stopped with his coffee cup halfway to his mouth. "Are you pulling my leg, Hank?"

I shrugged. "Come to the game today and see."

"Oh, I'll be there. That's my job—to report on the game for the folks back in New York."

I swallowed hard. "Are you that Damon?"

"Damon Runyon of the *American*."

Damon Runyon was the most famous sportswriter in the country. "And you came all the way from New York to see the Giants play a spring training game?"

Runyon laughed. "No, Hank. I came to see Babe Ruth get ready for the season. My readers want to know everything from what he eats for breakfast to what kind of knot he ties in his shoelaces. But I think they may be interested in Bill Pennant, too. Is the lion ready to lie down with the lamb yet?"

I don't know what got into me. I guess I was over-excited that Damon Runyon, a man I had been reading in the sports pages for as long as I could remember, was paying attention to me. I blurted, "He follows me around the bases."

"Really? And when can I witness this wonder?"

"Right before the game today. Just as the Giants take the field."

Runyon hopped off his stool. "Well, Hank, I'll be watching. See you at the ballpark."

Crowd
Pleasers

As soon as Runyon had gone, it hit me how foolish I had been. I didn't know from moment to moment if Bill would treat me like an old friend or an overdue meal. I had promised to deliver more than I had any right to expect.

I choked down the rest of my breakfast, even though I couldn't taste it anymore, and told the counterman to put it on the Giants' account. I hoped Smoky hadn't been teasing when he'd said I could do it. The counterman said, "Mr. Runyon paid for yours, son," heading off that problem.

I hustled back to Bears Stadium. Smoky had laid out a uniform for me in front of an empty locker, but eager as I was to put it on, I thought I had better tend to Bill Pennant first. In a few more hours, he had to behave like my buddy, or I would look like a fool.

Soon as I opened his door, Bill started rubbing my ankles. That was encouraging. I gave him some sardines, and he went to work on them. While he was busy, I put on the Giants uniform for the first time since September. We were wearing our home whites, with a fancy NY in orange on the left sleeve and on the cap. The flannel was as scratchy as ever, but nothing felt better than dressing like a big-leaguer.

I stuffed my clothes into the locker and slammed the door. Bill Pennant trotted over to me. I started toward the field, confident that he would follow. Instead, that fool cat squatted in front of my locker, batting at the door with his paw.

"Psst, psst, come on, Billy," I called. He ignored me, so I bent to pick him up. Mistake. Bill whirled and gave me a swat with one of those huge paws of his. Then he sat, his back against my locker, hissing and spitting.

I went into the equipment room and grabbed an extra set of catching gear. When I returned, wearing shin guards, chest protector, and face mask, I called Bill's name to make sure he recognized me.

Bill Pennant stood on his hind legs, scratching my locker with his claws. He stopped to sneer at me, then went back to stripping paint. I sighed and made a grab for the fur on his neck, hoping to pick him up and pin him against the chest protector.

That cat moved quicker than I could see. He leaped, and only the catcher's mask saved me. I was running around the locker room, Bill Pennant hanging from the bars of the mask, when the team arrived.

"Why don't you and Bill play in his room?" John McGraw said, peeling Billy off the catcher's mask. With a gentle nudge, he pushed me into the closet, half tossed the cat onto a shelf, and closed the door.

Bill ignored me, spending the next ten minutes bouncing off the walls. I took off the catcher's gear. When the players had dressed and left to warm up, Smoky knocked. "You can come out now, Hank. You need sardines to distract Bill?"

I would have loved to escape, but Runyon was waiting. Who knew how many other reporters he had told about my bragging? There were thirteen daily newspapers in New York City alone, and I stood a chance of looking like a fool in every one of them. So I said, "No, Smoky. I'm going to bring Bill Pennant with me."

"I'm out of here," Smoky said. I gave him a minute to make his escape, then opened the door. Bill sped straight to my locker and began clawing it again. The only thing in there was the smelly outfit I'd been wearing since I left New York.

Then it hit me. I had spilled fish oil on those clothes. It wasn't me Bill Pennant had followed around the base paths, but the aroma of sardines. I got a new can from Smoky's desk and keyed it open. Bill was on me in a flash. Before he decided to slice my leg into strips and eat it, I plucked the sardines from the can with my fingers and tossed them onto the floor. While Bill used his tongue like a wet mop, I took the can, still half filled with oil, into the dugout.

The Giants were seated on the bench while the

Yankees took batting practice. Usually the players would be honing their bats, rubbing saddle soap into their gloves, cleaning dirt from their cleats, or picking their teeth—anything except watching the other team. Today, all eyes were on the field.

A man who had to be Babe Ruth stood in the on-deck circle, leaning on a massive bat. He reminded me of a champion racehorse, all bulging muscle through the chest and shoulders, with the whole affair balanced on top of legs that looked too spindly to do the job. His unusual build, according to the Spalding Guide, was what gave him the combination of speed and power that so few players possessed.

The batter bunted, a signal that his twenty swings were finished, and ran to first base. Ruth hiked up his pants and strode to the plate, bat resting on his shoulder. The crowd let out a roar as if it were the last game of the year and the pennant was on the line. The players leaned forward in anticipation. Only McGraw lowered his head to his lineup card as if nothing Ruth did could interest him.

Babe lunged at the first pitch and hit a weak grounder. I noticed right away that he held the bat at the very end. You couldn't even see the knob sticking out. And his bat was huge. Could Babe Ruth really catch up with a good fastball swinging that thing?

Babe took a mighty cut at the second pitch, nearly corkscrewing himself into the ground on the follow-through. He popped it up, but what a pop-up! The crowd laughed as the infielders seemed to wait forever for the ball to come down. Ruth had the bugs excited over what would have been an easy out.

Then Babe smacked a long fly ball. Hit that high, I thought it would be another out. But the ball kept rising. It was still gaining altitude as it cleared the right field fence. The bugs leaped to their feet and let out a scream of joy as the ball went over the stands and into the street. My mouth dropped open. It hadn't seemed that Ruth had hit the ball that hard, and he had whacked it out of the ballpark.

That was the start of the greatest show of hitting I had ever seen. Ruth jumped on those batting-practice fastballs like Bill Pennant attacking a can of sardines. He hammered shots that banged off the wooden walls with an echoing jolt louder than the bugs' cheers. He launched three more of those long, graceful fly balls that soared past anything I had imagined in my baseball daydreams.

When Babe squared to bunt, then trotted to first base, the bugs stood as one and cheered until the ballpark shook. Babe gave the slightest touch to the brim of his cap as he disappeared into the Yankee dugout.

The Yankees were running off the field. McGraw hadn't ordered his boys out there yet. I figured he was waiting for the crowd to quiet so they could produce a fresh cheer for the Giants. This was my chance.

"Mr. McGraw," I called, "can me and Billy lead the team out?"

He looked surprised, but said, "Follow Hank, men," circling his arm over his head.

"Just give me a second to get Billy," I said, ducking into the locker room. Art Fletcher pulled his legs up onto the bench for protection.

Billy was halfheartedly licking a now shiny section of the floor. I drizzled a thin stream of oil leading to the dugout. Then, with a sigh at staining my new uniform, I poured the rest of the oil onto my pants legs and bolted for the field.

Taken by surprise, Bill hustled to catch up. That was just what I wanted. I touched home plate, then started around the bases. Billy caught me before I reached first and threw himself against my legs. I managed to keep my balance and made the turn toward second.

The bugs had been stunned to silence. But when Bill yowled in frustration and jumped for me as I rounded the second base bag, they whooped with laughter. For a few strides, that cat clung to the seat of my pants. Either the noise of the crowd or my running shook Bill off as I reached third base. I looked over my shoulder to see him land in the dirt, roll over, and start after me.

I let it all out and almost made home plate before Bill leaped on me again. This time I slowed and let him hang on as I trotted into the dugout. The bugs went crazy, and the Giants took the field. McGraw pulled Bill off and clapped me on the shoulder. "Attaboy, Hank. A wildcat tops a big ape any day at pleasing a crowd."

With Bill Pennant locked in the closet, I joined Smoky on the Giants' bench. Whether it was the noisy crowd or the rivalry between teams that shared a stadium, this game was different than most spring training outings.

McGraw managed as if it were midseason, pacing the dugout between pitches.

To the crowd's disgust, and McGraw's delight, Ruth struck out swinging at a slow curve his first time up. When George Burns singled to lead off the third, I knew a play would be on. Sure enough, George was off and running on the first pitch to Larry Doyle. Doyle came through with a base hit to right field, and the Giants had runners on the corners with no one out. Frankie Frisch, the young third baseman, was next. He pushed a bunt past the pitcher's mound, scoring Burns. A single by another rookie, Lee King, plated a second run before the inning was over.

Ruth was greeted with an even bigger roar on his next trip to the plate. He batted in the fourth inning, with a man on second. Fred Toney, the Giants' pitcher, didn't throw a single pitch he could reach. Taking the fourth ball, Ruth shook his head and trotted to first while the crowd booed Toney without mercy. Toney got Roger Peckinpaugh to pop up to retire the side. McGraw met him at the dugout steps and said, "Smart pitching, Fred."

Toney came back with, "Long as I don't have to run for election in San Antonio, I'll be all right." That got a laugh from all of us.

The seventh inning rolled around. A young right-hander named Virgil Barnes was on the mound for the Giants. His brother Jesse had won twenty-five games last year and figured to be McGraw's ace again this season. Everyone was hoping Virgil would come through, too.

This was probably the first time Virgil had pitched in

front of a big, noisy crowd. He got two outs on hard grounders, but walked two men in between. That brought Babe Ruth to the plate. Oh, how that crowd howled with greed and pleasure. It didn't matter which team they favored. Every bug wanted to see the Babe smack one.

Virgil was none too eager to pitch. He stalled, smoothing the dirt with his cleats, rubbing the baseball, and adjusting his cap. I think he was hoping that if he waited long enough, folks would get bored and go home. But the more he fidgeted, the more frantic the bugs got.

Ruth let the first pitch go for a called strike. Then Barnes tried to sneak a fast one by at the knees. Ruth dropped his bat on that ball and yanked it. Pep Youngs was playing right field, and he didn't even bother to move. He simply turned his head to watch the ball slam into the scoreboard at the top of the stands.

When I looked for the Babe, he was still standing at home plate, admiring his work. There was something about the power and grace of that swing, and the way Babe was enjoying himself that made me grin—until I saw John McGraw.

McGraw's face was purple. He came to the top step of the dugout and yelled, "Get moving, you big ape." The crowd was so loud that I don't know if Ruth heard him. At last, Babe circled the bases, using small steps to make the journey last.

Barnes got the next batter to end the inning. When the Yankees took the field, Ruth and most of the other regulars stayed in the dugout. Subs and rookies—what McGraw called yannigans—would play the rest of the afternoon. The bugs started to find their way to the exits.

No one seemed to care how the game would turn out. They had seen Babe Ruth hit a home run. Now it was time to go home and tell the family about it.

I didn't see Damon Runyon again that day. By the time I was done helping to store the equipment and clean up the locker room, the reporters had hammered out their stories and left.

Headliner
Hank

The next morning Bill Pennant was clawing the legs of my uniform pants as I ran the bases. We were skidding around second when I spotted Smoky at home plate waving a newspaper. "Hank, come read about yourself," he called.

That got my attention, but no way could I stop to read. I grinned and said, "Be right back," as I raced for Bill's closet. I got inside all right, but no matter what I did, I couldn't break his grip on my pants. At last I gave up and shrugged out of them. Billy had them pinned in a corner when I slipped out the door.

"You're lucky Mr. Runyon ain't here now," Smoky said, having followed me into the locker room. "He'd be bound to find amusement for his readers in this situation."

I went into Smoky's office and grabbed my civilian

pants. I had washed them out the night before, and they were still a little damp. But it beat running around in my skivvies, so I pulled them on. "I didn't know they sold the *American* here," I said.

"They don't, but the local papers pick up columns from out of town if they're about San Antone."

I sat on the edge of his battered desk, and Smoky handed me the newspaper. There was a picture of Babe Ruth, but I'll admit that I skipped down the page to a story headlined "Hank Cobb and Bill Pennant—McGraw's Latest Charm." *Last season, young Hank Cobb served the Giants in a variety of capacities, notably mascot and bat boy. This year you can add wild animal trainer to his resume. John McGraw has charged Hank with training the latest addition to the team, a Mexican wildcat optimistically named Bill Pennant.*

Yesterday Cobb displayed his progress, speeding around the bases with Bill Pennant in hot pursuit. At first it appeared that the two youngsters were engaged in a race. But when four legs inevitably caught two, the tableau more closely resembled hunter and prey in the wild. Bill Pennant dug his claws into Cobb's uniform and did his best to bring him down.

Cobb, however, met this challenge with his usual pluck, never slowing until he had crossed home plate. If McGraw can field a team as swift and scrappy as Hank Cobb and Bill Pennant, the Giants may indeed terrorize the league this season.

"How does it feel to read about yourself?" Smoky wondered.

It felt strange. Runyon had a way of making fun of you

31

that you didn't mind. "I guess I should thank Runyon," I told Smoky.

"He and the other reporters left town with Babe Ruth. We'll see them in Florida in a week or so."

The next few days drove the last thoughts of school out of my mind. The Giants played a slew of games—some against major-league teams, others against local colleges. Each day was hotter than the last, and I couldn't get enough of that Texas sunshine.

A strange thing happened when the Chicago White Sox came to town. I asked John McGraw to introduce me to some of the players, especially their ace pitcher Eddie Cicotte and the great Shoeless Joe Jackson. McGraw said, "Stay away from them," and stomped off.

I told Smoky about it. "All I know," Smoky said, "is that ever since Mr. McGraw went to the World Series, he's got nothing good to say about anybody on that Chicago team." So I stayed in my own dugout. It sure was fun to watch Shoeless Joe hit a baseball. I could see why the Spalding Guide said that he had the smoothest swing in the big leagues.

Before I knew it, it was time to wind our way toward New York and the start of the season. We would travel by rail from San Antonio, Texas, to Tampa Bay, Florida, for a rematch with Babe Ruth and the Yankees.

After sneaking into boxcars for years, riding as a paying passenger was one of my favorite parts of traveling with the Giants. A fellow had time to relax and listen to the pros talk baseball. I couldn't wait to board the train.

Smoky walked in that afternoon carrying a wooden crate with a screen across one end. "This here's Bill Pennant's berth for the trip. If he's done his business, load him inside."

Smoky made it sound easy. Bill and I were getting along all right, as long as I was feeding him, or at least smelled like food. I had a feeling he wasn't going to like being locked in a box. Two hooks held the screened end in place, and I popped them out of their eyes and swung the door open. Then I lined the inside of the crate with the oily pair of baseball pants that Bill had worn ragged with his claws.

I opened the closet door and started keying a can of sardines. Billy shot out after me. I snapped the lid off and threw the can into the travel crate. Bill got as far as the doorway and slammed on the brakes, his claws digging a new set of gouges in the wooden floor. He stuck his head in the crate and sniffed.

I reached down to push him from the rear, something I should have known better than to even try. Bill whirled and batted my hand with his right forepaw. He kept his claws sheathed, which I took as a sign of affection.

Keeping a wary eye on me, Bill flattened himself on the floor and snaked a paw into the crate. Cats are rubbery, but he couldn't quite reach the food. I was feeling pretty clever that I had chucked the can all the way to the back.

I still haven't figured out if Bill was smarter than me or if he was frustrated and got lucky. That cat dug his claws into the old uniform pants that lined the crate and scrabbled away at them. The sardine-covered pants bunched up in the doorway.

I rubbed my eyes. Bill gave me a smug look and dug in. He was picking through the cloth for spilled sardines when I got an idea of my own. I pulled the pants over him, shoved him hissing and spitting inside, and hooked the door. Either Smoky had built it strong or Bill didn't have enough space to gather momentum, because the door held no matter how many times he crashed into it.

I was slumped on the floor, trying to catch my breath and ignore the enraged snarls from the caged cat, when the players arrived. There was a flurry of activity as they emptied their lockers and threw on their uniforms. Then McGraw, already fully dressed, came in.

"Get a move on it, men. Parade starts in five minutes," he announced. Then he turned to me. "Afternoon, Hank. Is Bill Pennant ready to march?"

Just then Bill succeeded in turning the crate on its side, an event he greeted with an ungodly yowl. His claws raked the screen. I hoped it wouldn't make them even sharper. "I think we had better keep him locked up," I answered.

McGraw looked disappointed. "At least walk next to me carrying the crate. If Bill's going to bring us luck, he's got to be close at hand."

I pulled on my uniform in two seconds flat and rolled my civilian clothes into a bundle. Smoky offered to take it to the train for me, since I had to carry Bill Pennant.

We formed up near home plate. John McGraw, Bill Pennant, and I would walk first with the team in double file behind us. Each player carried a bat over one shoulder the way a soldier would tote a rifle. We marched across the diamond and out through the center field gate.

Both sides of South Presa Street were lined with bugs. When they caught sight of us, they let go a roar that startled Bill Pennant into action. I had all I could do to hang on to the crate as he flung himself around inside it. John McGraw marched proudly, a touch of his cap his only acknowledgment of the crowd.

By the time we reached the station, my arms were a couple of inches longer than they had been when I woke up. I set the crate on the wooden platform alongside the railroad tracks and worked at rubbing the ache out of my shoulders. I couldn't wait to get on board and flop down in my berth for a nap.

McGraw and the players piled into a car. Smoky put a hand on my shoulder when I tried to follow. "Your berth is down this way."

My heart sank. Smoky picked up Bill Pennant's crate and led me toward the rear of the train. We stopped at an open baggage car, and I looked inside. The car was divided into two barred and screened sections with locking doors. It reminded me of some of the jails the old man had overnighted in during our travels. An open aisle ran down the middle.

One section was piled high with the team's equipment. The other was empty. Smoky opened it and set Bill's crate inside. Then he handed me the key and said, "You can keep Billy in his travel box or let him loose, as long as he's behind bars."

"Do I have to stay here with him?"

Smoky pointed to a hammock strung across the center aisle, attached to the bars of each cell. "He's your roomie. Don't worry, I won't let either of you starve."

Smoky brought sardines for Billy and a steak with fried potatoes for me. My meal came with a silver dome over the plate and silverware wrapped in a cloth napkin. Fancy stuff. I would rather have been chomping on a chicken leg in the dining car with the ballplayers for company.

Billy raked the door of the crate while I got his dinner ready. The second I undid the first hook, he forced his way through the opening. Instead of racing for his bowl, he wheeled and attacked the crate's door with teeth and claws. By the time he collapsed on the floor, worn out by his frenzy, the mesh was torn and the door too mangled to close. He rested for a minute, then got up, groomed his fur, and sauntered over to his dinner. Before digging in, he gave me a look that clearly said, "Don't ever lock me in a box again."

I sat on the floor, an upturned packing crate serving as my dinner table. The train lurched to a start, dumping a few of my potatoes. Then the ride smoothed out. Bill did something I hadn't seen before. He walked away from his dish while there was still food in it. He wobbled across the cell, pressed his face against the mesh, and stared at me as if wondering what I had done to him this time.

I felt kind of down myself. When my father and I wandered the country, we used to hide in boxcars to sneak a free ride. There was no conversation. The old man didn't talk unless he was bossing me around.

Headliner Hank

Then I had hooked up with Chief Sunrise. Once he pitched his way onto the Giants, we rode in style. Chief was quiet, too, but in a more comfortable way. Even when the other players wanted nothing to do with us, we could listen to the great baseball yarns they told each other. Now I was back to having no one to talk to.

I lay in the hammock, the rhythm of the rails gently rocking me. The more I thought about it, the more Bill Pennant reminded me of the old man. I was there to keep him fed. Anytime I did something he didn't like, he'd light into me. Bill was in the cell, and I was on the outside. But who was really in charge? Would I even be with the team if it weren't for Bill Pennant?

I fell asleep and dreamed that the old man was in the cell. It was time for me to feed him, but he wouldn't move back from the door. I was afraid that if I opened it, he'd grab me instead of the food. I woke in a cold sweat, wondering how my father could scare me when he was in prison and I was free.

The train's brakes squealed, and I sat up fast, causing the hammock to sway. I gripped the sides and held on until I got my balance. Hopping down, I rubbed my eyes with one hand and used the other to scratch all those spots that itch in the morning.

By the time I had spit into my palms and smoothed back my hair, I was in front of Bill's cell. Bill Pennant lay on the floor as still as road kill.

Tape Measure
in Tampa Bay

Bug-eyed, I lifted the latch and slid the baggage car door along its track. I jumped to the station platform and slipped between Frankie Frisch and a young lady passenger he was chatting up. Smoky stepped down from the dining car with another of those silver-domed dishes that made each meal a surprise.

"Smoky, it's Bill. Come quick," I called.

Smoky never hurries, but he did lengthen his stride. "What's the matter, Hank?"

"He's not moving."

I raced back to the baggage car, vaulted through the doorway, and sped over to Bill's cell. He lay with his jaw flat on the floor. Smoky gave a low whistle when he came up behind me.

I unlocked the door, and Smoky went in, keying the

lid off a can of sardines. Bill Pennant ignored him. Smoky touched his back without losing a finger. "He don't feel hot, so there's no fever," he said. The steam whistle blew, and the train lurched to a start. Bill let out a low moan.

"You know what's wrong with this critter?" Smoky asked. I shook my head. "Motion sickness. He's not used to the world moving while he's standing still. Maybe by the time we get to Florida, he'll find his traveling legs. Leave water and food for him, and keep the door locked in case he starts feeling frisky."

At the next stop, Smoky rejoined the team, taking the dirty dishes from my ham-and-egg breakfast. Bill Pennant's stomach was empty, but his body wouldn't believe it. That poor cat dry heaved the rest of the trip to Tampa Bay.

As soon as we reached the station, John McGraw showed up. "Walk Billy to the ballpark, Hank. Two blocks down and take a left." He scooped Bill Pennant from the floor and handed him to me. Bill tucked his head under my arm and went to sleep, too exhausted to resist. I grabbed the travel crate in my free hand.

I was almost to the ballpark, when I heard a familiar voice. "Hey, lion tamer, is it safe to come near you?" Damon Runyon crossed the street to meet me, hands in pockets, porkpie hat riding low on his forehead.

"It's safe today. Bill Pennant's not feeling good."

Runyon reached out to pet him, then pulled back. I guess he was thinking how hard it would be to type with one hand. "What's wrong with him, Hank?"

"Smoky thinks he's motion sick."

Runyon laughed. "The ferocious beast is tamed by a train ride. Better hope he gets used to the railroad or he won't make much of a mascot."

I hadn't thought of that. If Bill Pennant couldn't travel, would McGraw take me along or send me back to school? That question scared me, so I changed the subject. "Thanks for the write-up."

"You earned it. Not everyone could steal the attention from Babe Ruth." Runyon nodded to a couple of men who had overtaken us. "Is McGraw still mad at the Babe for the way he strolled around the bases after that home run?"

Runyon's question made me realize how little I had been around John McGraw. I wouldn't have given him inside information anyway, but it felt bad not to know the answer. "You'll have to ask him that," I said.

Runyon laughed. "You sound like a veteran already. If you get a chance, stop up in the crow's-nest later. See what the game looks like from where I sit."

"Thanks, Damon. But I'll probably be busy in the dugout."

We reached the gate to Mayor's Field. Runyon said, "Bill Pennant, I hope you're feeling better next time I see you—as long as you're in a cage. Loose, I like you this way."

I took Billy into the locker room and waited for the others to arrive. I didn't know where we were going to keep him, but when I set the hated travel crate on the floor, Billy crawled into it and fell asleep. I guess he didn't mind it now that he had done away with the door.

The rookies and I carried a ton of uniforms and equipment into the ballpark. Smoky took charge of arranging things. I had hoped to be bat boy, but a local kid had that job sewed up. I set Billy's crate in a closet and closed the door. Then I went looking for Damon Runyon.

I was staring at the stands, trying to figure out where the crow's-nest was, when I heard someone calling my name. Runyon stood in the top row of the center field bleachers, waving his hat. I trotted down the left field line and climbed up and across the bleachers. By the time I got to the top, I was breathing hard.

"Best view in the house, Hank," Runyon said. He passed me a pair of binoculars, and I trained them on the Yankee dugout, hoping for a look at Babe Ruth. Shortstop Roger Peckinpaugh was easy to recognize. He was the most bowlegged player in the big leagues. It didn't seem to slow him down on the bases, though. I saw a squatty man in shin guards that had to be Muddy Ruel, the catcher. I didn't see Babe or anyone else I knew, so I passed the glasses back to Runyon.

"Babe's probably inside, resting up for the game," Runyon said. "Rumor is he missed bed check last night."

"Will he be allowed to play?" I asked.

"Oh yeah. Miller Huggins, the Yankees manager, knows that most everyone is here to see the Babe. He's not going to make all these people angry just to prove a point."

Sure enough, when the Yankees took the field, Ruth was with them. I followed him with the glasses until he reached his position in left field, swept his cap from his

41

head, and bowed to the crowd. I wondered if McGraw saw him. If so, he'd be burned up. He expected players to ignore the bugs and go about their business.

The Giants went out one-two-three, as if they, too, were eager to see Ruth hit. Fred Toney retired the first two Yankees. Then Wally Pipp singled, bringing the Babe to the plate.

Toney threw the first pitch right at him. Ruth dropped to the ground, barely escaping. The crowd lit into Toney, calling him names even I hadn't heard before. I felt bad for Fred. I knew the knockdown had been ordered by John McGraw.

Runyon leaned forward in his seat. "Let's see how the big man reacts to that."

The Babe took his time settling into the batter's box. I focused in close, and it looked like he might strangle that huge bat of his. Toney threw a fastball, and Ruth stepped into it, meeting the ball with every ounce of his strength.

Runyon let out a gasp as the ball soared higher and higher. It passed over our heads, and, I swear, the ball was still rising. I whipped around in time to see it land clear across the street from the ballpark and bounce through the open door of a cigar store. Surely no one had ever hit a baseball that far before.

Runyon said, "Hank, did you see where it landed?" I nodded, still not able to speak. "Mark the spot. After the game, you and I are going to figure out how far that ball went."

The bugs threatened to knock the ballpark down with

their shouts. I turned as Babe was rounding third base. I thought he might say something to Toney. Instead, he stared into the Giants' dugout. Through the binoculars I saw John McGraw, his head lowered over his lineup card.

Babe batted once more, lining out to second base. When he didn't take the field to start the fourth inning, the fans booed halfheartedly. No one could muster a real complaint after what they had been privileged to witness. The rest of the afternoon, the bugs seated near us spent as much time staring across the street at the spot where Babe's home run had landed as they did watching the game. If you're going to do something miraculous, there's nothing like having a few thousand witnesses.

The score was 8–8 after nine innings, rookies alternating between good plays that gave you hope for the future and boneheaded mistakes that made you wonder how they had gotten this far. McGraw and Huggins met at home plate, shook hands, and agreed to leave the game tied. The fans had been trickling out for an hour or more, and there were as many across the street looking back at the ballpark as there were in the stands.

Everyone else filtered out through the center field gate. Runyon and I crossed the diamond. "Ask Smoky for a tape measure," he said.

I trotted off. Smoky always carried a tape in his pocket so he could fit players for their uniforms. I couldn't see how it would help us much, being only about five feet long. Were we going to crawl across the field, laying the tape out between us?

Smoky grinned. "Is Runyon trying to measure that

43

home run? Better take this, too." He dug into a canvas bag and pulled out a ball of twine. Tape in one hand, twine in the other, I ran to meet Runyon at home plate.

"My stride is almost exactly a yard long, Hank. First we'll see how many strides to the center field fence." We counted silently as Runyon paced off the distance. When his right toe bumped the outfield fence, he turned to me.

"One hundred twenty," I announced.

"That's what I got, too. Times three, makes 360 feet to here."

We went into the stands and stood in the front row of the bleachers. Runyon used the tape to learn that the rows of bleachers were two feet apart. We counted thirty rows up to our seats.

"Thirty times two is another sixty feet," I said.

"That makes 420, so far," Runyon said, staring toward home plate.

"How does he do it?" I asked.

"He's strong. He swings a fifty-four-ounce bat, where most players use one weighing less than forty ounces." Runyon stopped to think. "And he's fearless. He swings with all his might every time. Babe's not afraid to look like a jackass when he misses."

I thought about it as we climbed down the bleachers and walked out onto the field and through the gate. Everything Runyon said made sense, but there had to be more to it.

Most major-leaguers were strong, and a few were as big as the Babe. If all it took was a heavier bat and a harder swing, I guessed a lot of players would be hitting the long ball.

Even if we had forgotten to mark the spot where the baseball had landed, it would have been easy to find. A mob stood in front of the cigar store, arms waving, fingers pointing, and tongues flapping with the story of the home run.

Runyon leaned against the ballpark wall, grabbed the loose end of the twine, and handed me the rest. "Run it out, Hank, and we'll see what we've got."

I waited for a Model T to chug past, then crossed the street, paying out string behind me. One of the bugs by the cigar store spotted me and elbowed another. He yelled into the open doorway of the store, and before I knew it, I was surrounded.

A man in a three-piece suit, cigars sticking out of the vest pockets, tapped me on the shoulder. "Are you figuring out how far that thing went?" he asked. "Had to be five hundred feet."

That started an argument. "Five hundred? More like eight hundred!"

"I say six hundred," added another.

"Maybe four fifty," threw in a fourth.

They stopped arguing about the number long enough to fight over the exact spot where the ball had landed. The man with the cigars settled that one. He pulled the baseball from a pants pocket. "I caught it on the first bounce as I walked to the doorway of my store for some fresh air. It landed right here."

He hawked up a phlegm ball and spat it on the sidewalk. I let out string to within an inch of the spot, pinched it between my fingers, and looked back at Runyon. He made a sign like a pair of scissors with two fingers of his free hand. The cigar salesman picked up on it. He reached in another pocket and came out with one of those gadgets men use to snip the end off a stogie. He cut the string, and Runyon began reeling it in. I ducked under a couple of elbows and made my escape, the frustrated bugs yelling at us for information.

Runyon handed me Smoky's tape measure, mumbled that he was on deadline, and hurried off to write his story. "Aren't you going to measure the string?" I called after him.

"More accurate at the hotel," he yelled over his shoulder.

Opening
Day

The next morning, when our train pulled into Jacksonville, I found a newspaper that carried the story. "Five hundred twenty-five feet!" I told Bill Pennant, putting as much oomph as I could into the number.

Billy was unimpressed. He lay flattened out behind bars in the baggage car, looking more dead than alive. He had eaten a couple of good meals while we were in Tampa Bay, and I had spent the first hour of our ride this morning scraping them off the floor. That left me feeling queasy myself. The condition he was in, the only thing Bill Pennant could inspire a ballplayer to do was throw up.

By the end of the week, we were in New York. The Giants had looked good the past few days and were chomping at the bit to start the season. The biggest changes from last year's squad were at first and third base.

Slick-fielding Hal Chase and Heinie Zimmerman were gone.

Frankie Frisch was a better third baseman than Zimmerman had ever been, and just as good a hitter. But the real spice he brought to the Giants was speed. The Fordham Flash was a great base runner.

The new first baseman, George Kelly, was nicknamed Highpockets because of his long legs. Being so tall, he wasn't the best at scooping throws out of the dirt, and he sometimes got his feet tangled when he had to rush to cover the bag. But Kelly could flat-out hit.

Best of all, the new players could be counted on to always play their best. Chase and Zimmerman were fonder of gambling than baseball. McGraw had kicked Chase off the team last September for trying to throw games. Zimmerman had been caught selling stolen auto parts over the winter. I didn't miss those guys, and I don't think any of the other Giants did, either.

I figured that within a week, Bill Pennant's future and mine would be decided. The Giants' season began with five games at the Polo Grounds. I was hoping that the team would come flying out of the gate, proving Bill's luckiness and putting John McGraw in a good mood. Then he might listen to a boy who wanted to travel with the team instead of going back to school.

McGraw had a zoo-type cage waiting for Bill Pennant at the Polo Grounds, so I didn't have to stand guard at night. The cage had a tree branch Bill could climb. It featured little doors I could stick my hand through to feed Billy and clean up any messes he made. His travel crate fit in one corner, in case he was in the mood for hiding. Once Billy realized that his new home wasn't going to wander the countryside, his stomach settled, and he was back to his old feisty self. I wouldn't have minded his sharpening his claws on the tree branch if he didn't have to eyeball me whenever he did it.

It was a pleasure to sleep in my comfortable bed at the Graham Court apartment. The McGraws went out almost every night, but I had plenty to do. After softening my mitt with saddle soap, I'd dig into the mountain of newspapers delivered to the apartment each day. For a guy who loves the comic strips as much as I do, that was a real treat. I caught up on old favorites like the *Katzenjammer Kids, Toonerville Trolley,* and *The Gumps,* and got hooked on a new one called *Barney Google.* Barney spent his time at racetracks, ballparks, and boxing arenas—all places I'd like to be. Wherever he went, he ended up in a jam. What I liked most about Barney was that he never gave up. No matter what happened to him, he jumped out of bed the next morning, eager to try again.

When I was done plowing through the comics, I'd hit the sports pages. Each paper had at least one columnist I enjoyed. I read Runyon first, of course, and he was tough to beat. But a fellow named Ring Lardner often made me laugh out loud. My only regret was not having Chief Sunrise around to share the fun. I kept my eyes peeled, but the papers seldom mentioned the Negro National League where Chief would compete this season.

Opening day came, and I hadn't made much progress

with Bill Pennant. He liked his new cage so much that he wasn't interested in coming out. John McGraw had promised the reporters that Billy would be on display, and you couldn't pick up a sports page without reading his name. I decided that the best way to guarantee Billy's cooperation was not to feed him on game day. While the players were getting dressed, he kept up a nonstop yowling. Every few minutes, he banged his food dish against the side of the cage, in case we didn't understand what he wanted.

By game time most every seat was taken. Our opponent was the Boston Braves, and their star shortstop, Rabbit Maranville, was the main attraction. The Rabbit was the best fielding shortstop in the game, and a character besides. He wore his hat sideways, turned every pop fly into an adventure with his below-the-waist basket catch, and never missed an opportunity for a laugh.

One game last season, Umpire Bill Klem was calling strikes on pitches that the Braves thought were too low. When it was Rabbit's turn to hit, he dropped to his knees in the batter's box. Fred Toney was pitching, and he got to laughing so hard that he couldn't throw a strike. When Klem called ball four, Rabbit shuffled all the way to first base on his knees. Even McGraw had to smile.

Warmups completed, the Braves ran into their dugout. Rabbit gave the bugs a thrill by turning a cartwheel down the steps. John McGraw caught my eye and said, "Is Bill Pennant ready to bring us some luck?" I nodded my head and ducked into the locker room to fetch him.

Taking no chances, I not only dumped fish oil on my

pants legs, but stuffed the sardines into the back pocket of my uniform. Billy was frantic with hunger. I unlatched one hook from the door of his cage, and he pushed his way through. I bolted for the field, a smile of relief lighting my face when he followed.

We raced around first and second as the fans cheered. I looked toward third and was amazed to see Rabbit Maranville standing on the bag waiting for us. Rabbit smiled and held up a paper bag for the crowd to see. He waited until Billy and I were close enough to smell his breath, then turned the bag upside down and shook it.

A tangle of mice landed at my feet. They scrambled in all directions, and Bill Pennant forgot about me. Here was a gourmet treat that easily outshone his daily diet of sardines. Plus he would have the fun of killing the meal himself.

Bill Pennant sped into the outfield, with me chasing him. Each time he got close to one mouse, he was distracted by another and shot off in a new direction. The bugs thought this was the funniest thing they had ever seen. I was glad Runyon was off covering the Yankees.

McGraw sent the rookies out to help me. O'Hara, the man in charge of maintenance who had hired me to wipe down seats the previous spring, showed up with a butterfly net. He never got close enough to throw it over Bill Pennant, or I'm sure Billy would have torn it to shreds. Finally, we managed to form a circle around Bill Pennant near the flagpole in deep center field. Smoky headed our way carrying Bill's travel crate. I stepped into the circle, hoping Billy would be attracted now that the mice had disappeared. Instead of coming to me, Bill scrambled up the flagpole.

Smoky joined me in gawking, our heads thrown back. That cat didn't stop until his claws dug into the wooden ball that decorated the top of the pole. He puffed out his fur and hissed down at us. McGraw was jawing with umpire Bill Klem. "Leave him up there," McGraw called when he got close enough to be heard. "Maybe he'll make the Braves nervous."

While McGraw and the rookies trotted to the dugout, and Smoky and O'Hara walked through the center field gate, I ran for the foul line. In previous seasons, the home team had been required to provide two new baseballs for each game. The owners had decided that using a dirty, beat-up ball gave the pitchers too big an advantage. So this year, the umpires were instructed to keep a clean ball in play at all times.

Problem was, that was expensive. A new baseball cost $2.50, and in spring training, teams had gone through as many as ten in one game. It was hard enough recovering balls hit into the stands. Lately, the bugs had taken to leaning over the railings and grabbing foul balls that bounced past.

My new job was to sit along the left field line and retrieve foul balls before the bugs could get them. I loved it, because it gave me a chance to flash some fancy glove work in front of the crowd. George Burns brought my mitt from the dugout and flipped it to me on his way to left field.

Jesse Barnes took the mound for the Giants and, for the first six innings, looked every bit the star. Barnes held the

Boston hitters in check while the Giants were pecking away for three runs. Bill Pennant seemed content to watch from his free seat, and after a while folks focused on the game instead of the flagpole.

In the seventh inning, things fell apart. A couple of walks, an error by Highpockets Kelly, and a double tied the score. Barnes settled and got two outs. Ray Powell, a lanky outfielder, was at bat. He hit a towering fly ball to deep center field. I wasn't worried. It would take a cannon to hit a ball over the center field fence at the Polo Grounds. I had seen Lee King run down balls like this many times in practice. Lee kept retreating and seemed to have the ball lined up, his back nearly touching the flagpole.

Everyone saw Lee take a quick look to see what Bill Pennant was up to. He claimed afterward that the cat hissed at him. But how he could hear that over the roar of the crowd, I don't know. The ball ticked off King's glove and rolled away. Boston had the lead, and Powell wound up on third base. Before the last out was recorded, he scored, too. The Giants never recovered, losing the opener 6–3. Bill Pennant had brought luck all right— bad luck.

When the game ended, I dug the battered sardines from my pocket and set them on the grass at the base of the flagpole, hoping they would lure Billy down. He stared at the clouds and ignored me. I turned and walked toward the dugout. Just as I reached the infield dirt, a blur of fur sped past me. I ran myself, figuring I would find Bill Pennant in his cage.

The sound of a baseball bat crashing into a locker

greeted me instead. A wild-eyed Lee King was chasing Bill Pennant around the locker room. Bill ran under a wooden bench and out the other side a second before a blow from the bat turned it into kindling wood. John McGraw popped out of his office, yelling King's name. Either Lee didn't hear or was too mad to care. He careened after Bill Pennant, bat cocked and ready.

I was standing at the bottom of the dugout steps, too startled to move. Bill Pennant sprang to the top of a locker, and from the locker into my arms. Lee King charged, and I think he would have smashed Billy and me, except that Smoky grabbed the barrel of the bat in his backswing. Players closed in and wrestled King to the floor.

Sweat ran down my face. Billy had sunk his claws into my chest, and I tried to coax him into letting go. John McGraw looked down at Lee King and snorted, "I don't like to lose, either. Why don't you see if you can take your anger out on those bean eaters tomorrow instead of wrecking our locker room?"

I was trying to pull Billy off my jersey, but he buried his head under my armpit and held on for dear life. Smoky said, "Keep him like that, Hank." He came back a minute later with Billy's collar. I lifted my arm, and Smoky looped the collar around Billy's neck, cinching it without a fight. I carried the cat to his cage, and when he saw the open door, he hopped in and hid in his travel crate. Hungry as he was, he didn't come out, even when I dropped a dish of sardines into the cage.

American
Flyer

ext day, John McGraw and I walked to the Polo Grounds in a steady drizzle. Spring had run off to hide, and the wind made it feel like March all over again. "The real fans will be in the stands today, Hank," McGraw said. If he was right, there weren't too many of them. The huge stadium was more than half empty, and the bugs that were on hand acted like they were too cold to make any noise.

Smoky helped me lure a hungry Bill Pennant from his cage. As soon as Billy stuck his head out the partially opened door, Smoky clipped the leash to his collar. While Bill Pennant ate the couple of sardines we used as bait, I wrapped the other end of the leash around my right hand. If that cat climbed any flagpoles today, he would have to take me with him.

When it came time for us to run the bases, McGraw stationed Highpockets Kelly in the third base coaching box, near the Boston dugout. If Maranville tried to pull another stunt, he would have Kelly to answer to. I dumped the rest of the sardines into my back pocket, fish oil running down my legs, and headed for the diamond.

The bugs were silent as I started toward first, Bill Pennant running to avoid being dragged by the leash. Halfway to the bag, he passed me. I sped up, but Billy ran between my legs and jumped for my pocket. The leash tripped me, and I sprawled headfirst in the baseline. That got a laugh from the bugs.

The more I struggled to get up, the more tightly Billy wound the leash around my legs. He clawed the sardines from my pocket and ate them off my rear end while the crowd roared.

I lay there in disgrace until the Giants took the field. John McGraw came out and grabbed Billy by the collar. He unclipped the leash and carried him back to his cage. The bugs jeered as I freed myself and ran to the dugout for my mitt. They jeered some more as I ran down the left field line. I was never more happy to see a game start, giving the bugs something else to think about.

Fred Toney was sensational for the Giants, pitching the whole nine innings, and giving up just one run. Problem was, New York didn't score at all. Boston hurler Joe Oeschger's pitches were as hard to hit as his name was to pronounce. It took just ninety minutes for the Giants to lose the game. I didn't see how anyone could blame Bill Pennant for this loss, but Lee King made a special trip down the hallway to spit into Billy's cage.

The Phillies came to town next, and in three games, the Giants scored a total of three runs. We were lucky to win the second game of the series, 2–1, behind Jesse Barnes. But leaving home with one win and four losses had everyone in a vile mood. John McGraw never asked for Bill Pennant, and I sure didn't volunteer, so the cat spent the series curled up in his cage.

My whole life, if things weren't going well in one town, I hopped a freight and tried somewhere else. There was nothing like travel to make a guy forget his problems. So I had to hold back a smile as I packed my road uniform after the last game of the series. We were heading for Boston, and I couldn't wait for a chance to get even with that bunch. McGraw passed through on the way to his office, and I asked, "What time does our train leave?"

He said, "The team leaves at seven in the morning, but you're staying here, Hank. Bill Pennant lives at the Polo Grounds, and you're his keeper. We don't have a home game for two weeks, and I hope by then you'll have Billy under control."

"I don't know if he can be trained," I mumbled.

"Would you rather go back to school? If you don't want your job, just say so. O'Hara will have his nephews lined up to compete for it."

My ears drooped thinking of all the excitement I would miss. But then I remembered something. While the Giants were on the road, Babe Ruth and the Yankees would be at the Polo Grounds. "I'll do my best, Mr. McGraw," I promised.

Next morning, I stayed in bed, listening to John McGraw thump around the apartment. I was sure that he would come and say good-bye. Maybe if I looked down-cast enough, he'd have a last-minute change of heart. When the door banged, I knew he had left without me. I was too hungry to mope, so I got dressed and went into the kitchen.

"Good morning, Hank. There's oatmeal on the stove," Mrs. McGraw greeted me.

"Did he leave?" I asked, even though I knew the answer.

"He's gone for five days, until they play the Robins in Brooklyn. He'll sleep here during that series."

As I dished up my oatmeal I said, "I thought he'd at least say good-bye."

"He was thinking of you," Mrs. McGraw said.

"Oh, sure."

"Finish your breakfast and we'll go down to the lobby together. Mr. McGraw has left a surprise for you."

That perked me up. I was sure it was a bat. Players were always squawking when I borrowed one of theirs. I shoveled that oatmeal down in record time, grabbed my cap and mitt, and bolted for the door.

The staircase at Graham Court is fancy enough to be in a movie theater. Because it's curved, I couldn't see the front doors until we were all the way down to the lobby. Then I froze, afraid to believe that what I saw was true.

A brand-new bicycle, black with white-sidewall tires and polished wooden rims sat next to Jimmy the door-man. "It's yours, Hank, a top-of-the-line American Flyer," Jimmy said when he spotted me. "Now you can ride back and forth to the Polo Grounds in style."

I shot across the lobby and ran my hand over the

smooth leather seat. A basket hung from the front of the handlebars, and I dropped my mitt into it. The Flyer had a flat-bottomed metal stand that snapped down from the rear wheel so the bicycle wouldn't fall over when you parked it. Jimmy lifted the stand and folded it behind the seat. "Do you know how to ride?" he asked.

I knew the idea of it, having seen other kids ride a million times. But I'd never tried myself. "I can figure it out," I said, pushing the cycle toward the doors.

"Oh no, you don't," Mrs. McGraw said, blocking my path. "You'll not go tooling around the streets of New York until I'm convinced that you know what you're doing."

"Where can I practice?"

Jimmy shrugged. "This lobby is big enough for a bicycle convention. Mrs. McGraw, if you'll be kind enough to stand at the bottom of the stairs to warn anyone who might come down, I'll help Hank."

I climbed in the saddle, finding it hard to believe that this beautiful machine was mine. Pumping the pedals, I set off around the lobby, wobbling but not falling, thanks to Jimmy's steadying hand on the back of the seat. We did three laps, and I felt a little more comfortable on each one. The fourth time I whipped past the front doors, Jimmy was standing there, wiping his sweaty face with a handkerchief. I was riding!

I circled the lobby a couple more times while Jimmy explained how to stop. "Press your feet backwards on the pedals. When you slow down, tilt to one side, and drop your foot to the floor."

It sounded easy. I jammed down both feet, and the

bicycle swerved. I would have fallen if I hadn't grabbed the banister at the bottom of the staircase. "Gently, Hank," Jimmy encouraged. "Ease into it, and you'll stop smoothly."

I had to stop five times without tipping over before Mrs. McGraw was satisfied. She gave Jimmy the nod, and he held the door open for me. I pushed the cycle across the sidewalk and into the street, grinning so wide that it hurt my mouth. Then I wobbled off toward the Polo Grounds, enjoying the breeze and only getting honked at twice the whole way.

I hopped off near the players' entrance, stopping just before running into the concrete wall of the stadium. I snapped down the stand and used my sleeve to polish the wooden rims and dust the fenders. Grabbing my mitt from the basket, I turned and banged on the door.

Just as I threw an imaginary baseball at it, O'Hara opened the door. He ducked, then smiled and said, "If you're here to wipe down the bleachers, you're too late. The rear ends of the bugs have them polished to a fine gloss."

I laughed. "I'm here to feed Bill Pennant."

"Good luck to you, Hank. Every time I get close to his cage, he spits and throws himself against the mesh. He won't be doing any flagpole climbing today, will he?"

"I sure hope not. I'm supposed to teach him to walk on a leash." O'Hara waved me inside. "Can I bring in my cycle?"

"Sure, where is it?"

I spun around. My brand-new American Flyer with its

polished wooden rims was gone. I looked up the street in time to see a cyclist lean right and whip around the corner. I threw O'Hara my mitt and took off running, not even waiting to see if he caught it. I tore to the end of the block, startling three old-timers clogging the sidewalk while they solved the world's problems. I ignored their complaints and flew around the corner, expecting my cycle to be long gone. Instead, it was parked alongside a hot dog wagon, the thief leaning off the seat to take a hot dog from the vendor.

"Hey, you!" I yelled. I know it was dumb, but I was running out of steam. The thief looked at me, tipped his hat with his free hand, and pedaled off, the hot dog hanging from his mouth.

Now I was too mad to be tired. I put my head down and tore up the sidewalk. I was gaining on him until he stood and pumped for all he was worth. He pulled away, nearly crashing as he made a right turn at high speed. By the time I rounded the corner, he was nowhere in sight.

I slumped on a stoop, chest heaving, and ground my knuckles into my temples in frustration. How was I going to explain to John McGraw? I looked longingly up the empty street as if wishing could make the cycle reappear. When my breathing slowed, I got up and trudged down the block. No matter how I felt, I had to take care of Bill Pennant.

My eyes were glued to the pavement. I was almost to the hot dog stand when a voice said, "A kid that can run like you doesn't need a bicycle."

My head popped up. There was the thief, sitting on

my machine. I charged, determined to knock him to the sidewalk where we would be the same size. Then I froze. The man astride my cycle was Babe Ruth. "How do you like your hot dogs, Kid?" he asked.

Batting
Practice

y head was spinning. I had been as low as a guy could get, and now I was on top of the world. Babe Ruth and I were pounding hot dogs down our throats and talking baseball. "Aren't the Yankees off today?" I managed to ask between bites.

"Manager gave us off," Babe said, stopping to chew, "but I'm in a slump. Thought I'd stop by the park and hit a few. You look like you could throw the ball over the plate, Kid. Want to pitch some?"

"I've got a job to do first," I said, "but it should only take ten minutes or so."

We walked to the Polo Grounds, me pushing the cycle so I could stay at Ruth's side. I knew from the newspapers that the Yankees were doing as poorly as the

Giants. They, too, had lost four of their first five games, and Babe had yet to hit a homer.

"People are calling me a bum—saying I stole the Yankees' money. But it's a long season, Kid. Soon as I find my stroke, I'll show them something," Babe said.

O'Hara let us in, returning my mitt. This time I wheeled the cycle into the locker room. I offered to introduce Babe to Bill Pennant, but he wasn't interested. "I meet enough wildcats in the evenings. Daytimes, I like to concentrate on baseball." He and O'Hara thought that was funny.

Usually, I spent some time making noises and staring into Billy's cage, hoping he'd be curious enough to come out of hiding. Today I dumped food into his dish, shoved it through the little door, and hurried to get into uniform. Carrying a canvas sack of baseballs in my right hand, and wearing my mitt on my left, I walked out to home plate.

Babe was kneeling in the on-deck circle, rubbing that enormous bat of his with an oily rag. He wore pinstriped uniform pants and an old sweatshirt that looked like he had used it for a napkin on more than one occasion. I warmed up by tossing a few against the stands from home plate. When my arm felt loose, I gathered the baseballs and carried the sack out to the mound.

Babe took his place in the batter's box and gazed at the right field fence, only 257 feet away at the foul line. "If the fence was this close in Boston, I'd have hit fifty home runs last year," he boasted.

I laughed to myself. The twenty-nine home runs he had hit was an unbelievable total. No one would ever hit

fifty. But I called out, "Go get 'em, Babe," and toed the rubber.

Babe noticed how I was dressed. "That Giants uniform is just the edge I need. I'm going to pretend that you're John McGraw and try to swat one right through you."

I wasn't scared. I've been ribbed often enough to know when it's happening. I took a deep breath to relax. I'd pitched to Chief Sunrise plenty of times. Why should it be any different with Babe Ruth? From what I'd read in the papers, he'd grown up as raggedy as me. Babe had a mother and father, but they were so busy running a saloon they owned in Baltimore that they didn't take care of him. When he got into trouble, they dumped him in an orphanage.

My first two pitches were wild, but from rust, not fear. Then I found the range, and Babe Ruth went to hacking. I lost track of how many balls he hit off the fence or into the seats. All I know is that each time the ball bag was empty, there were fewer baseballs on the field for me to round up.

Gathering baseballs gave me time to think. Babe seemed to do everything the opposite of what John McGraw recommended. Instead of choking up, he gripped the bat at the end. I'd been taught to hit down on the ball, to get it on the ground before a fielder could catch it. Babe's swing was an uppercut. He wanted to hit the ball in the air.

Whether I pitched in on his fists or away, Babe pulled the ball toward the short fence in right field. I had learned that it was smart baseball to stroke outside pitches to the opposite field. Babe didn't want singles. He tried to hit the ball as hard and as far as he could, every time he swung the bat. Maybe McGraw had to scrap for every edge because he was small. If I kept growing, why couldn't I hit like the Babe?

There were only half a dozen baseballs left when Babe announced that he had had enough. "I feel good now, Kid. Think I'll save some long ones for the game tomorrow."

He disappeared into the dugout while I headed for right field to collect the few remaining baseballs. By the time I came in, he was gone, his stained sweatshirt hanging from the lip of a garbage barrel in a corner of the locker room. O'Hara took the ball bag and hefted it in his hand. "Looks like the Yankees are going to go through some baseballs this season. Have you got time to round up the ones in the seats?"

I had the whole afternoon. Babe had hit a few balls out of the park, but most of his shots were hiding under empty seats and benches. I walked the stands from the right field line to right center and nearly filled the bag.

Now I had no excuse not to work with Bill Pennant. I dumped some fish oil on Babe's old sweatshirt and tied it around my waist. Holding the leash in one hand, I opened Bill's cage. Instead of bursting out, he scrambled down the tree branch and into his crate.

I stuck my mitt into the doorway, just to see what would happen. One paw flashed out, leaving a tear in the leather. That discouraged me from trying to reach in and clip the leash to his collar. It looked like we weren't going to run the bases today. I locked Bill's cage and left. Riding home on the American Flyer, I laughed out loud picturing myself chasing Babe Ruth down the street.

Next morning, I got to the park early. Babe Ruth was the only Yankee I knew, and I wasn't sure how his teammates would react to a kid in a Giants uniform hanging around the locker room. I had fed Bill Pennant and was sitting on a bench in front of my locker rubbing saddle soap into my mitt, when a voice said, "Is your name Hank?"

I whipped around to find a pipsqueak in a suit and tie standing behind me, hands on hips. "Hank Cobb," I admitted. "Who's asking?"

"I'm Miller Huggins. I hear you spent some time with Babe Ruth yesterday." I couldn't believe my ears. This flyspeck was the manager of the Yankees? Their owner must be crazy to think that Babe Ruth and the rest of those monsters would listen to this squirt.

When I stood to shake hands, I saw that Huggins was a little shorter than me, about the same height as John McGraw. But McGraw was all beef and muscle. This character was skin and bone. He looked like he had to put rocks in his pockets on windy days. But I was polite, since he was the man in charge. "Yes, sir. I threw batting practice. He smacked some beauties."

"I'm sure. Look, Hank, for whatever reason, Babe Ruth likes you. He's been known to get into trouble off the field. He eats too much, goes places he shouldn't, and . . . indulges in a few bad habits I'd rather not mention."

"Whiskey and women?" I asked.

Huggins squirmed. "Let's just say he's not always at his best when he gets to the ballpark."

I knew how John McGraw would handle the Babe. If he showed up having eaten or drunk too much, McGraw would put him through his paces until he collapsed or lost his lunch. Then he'd sit him on the bench until he begged to get back in the lineup.

"O'Hara tells me that you'll be here every day."

"I will."

"I'd consider it a personal favor if you hung around with Ruth as much as possible. Keep him busy when there's no game. The Yankees will make it worth your while."

Was he offering to pay me to spend time with Babe Ruth? Any kid in America would cough up his own money for the chance. "I'm on the Giants' payroll already, Mr. Huggins. If Babe will put up with me, I'm your man."

Huggins stroked his chin. "We can't have you sitting in the dugout dressed like that." He stood next to me, taking my measure. "I bet you'll fit into one of my old uniforms."

I followed Huggins into his office. It was half the size of McGraw's. Maybe that's why the Yankees hired such a small manager. The two of us squeezed inside, and he shut the door. A half-dozen Yankee uniforms hung from a rod mounted on one wall. Huggins pulled down the uniform on the far end, handed it to me, and said, "Welcome to the squad, Hank."

I gave a feeble smile. It was starting to dawn on me that John McGraw might not be happy if he knew I was running around in a Yankee uniform. But, hey, if it were up to me, I'd be in Boston with the Giants. If this was the only way I could spend my days in a big-league dugout, so be it. Besides, McGraw might never find out.

The uniform fit—sort of. I spent so much time pulling down the pants and yanking on the sleeves that it looked like I was giving signals. Being in the Yankee dugout made me even more twitchy. It was two-thirty, only an hour before game time, and Babe Ruth hadn't shown up yet.

Most of the players ignored me, the way the Giants had last season. I knew not to take it personally. But Carl Mays, a pitcher who had come over from the Red Sox in a trade, was downright nasty. "What the hell are you doing here?" he asked.

"Mr. Huggins invited me," was the best I could come up with.

"Stay out of my way," Mays said, shoving past me to jog in the outfield. I put up with his lip. But I suspected that before too many more seasons passed, I'd be a strapping six-footer like he was. Maybe then I'd put him in his place with my bat.

I was running down foul balls in batting practice, trying to make myself useful, when Huggins waved me over. "He's here," he said and jerked his head toward the locker room.

I wasn't sure what I was supposed to do, but I ran off the field and down the dugout steps. I found the Babe in the locker room with his head in a sink, cold water raining on his skull. He stayed under so long that I thought he might be drowning himself. Then he stood up straight and shook his head from side to side like a dog leaving a pond. Water sprayed everywhere.

Babe spotted me. "Morning, Kid."

"Afternoon, Babe," I answered.

"I see you're on the team. I told Huggins you were a good man, straightened out my swing."

"He's not too happy right now, Babe. You missed batting practice."

"Tell Little Man I'm ready. I warmed up yesterday with you. Don't want to waste any more good strokes."

By the time I got back to the dugout, the Yankees were sitting while their opponents, the Philadelphia Athletics, warmed up. The A's had a glorious past, winning the World Series three times between 1910 and 1913. When he was loaded, my old man liked to rattle off the lineup of those teams. Now the A's were the sorriest bunch in the majors.

After the 1913 season, the players demanded raises. Their owner and manager, Connie Mack, got so mad that he sold his champion baseballers to other teams. He promised the Philadelphia bugs that he would build a new powerhouse with young players. Since then, the A's had finished in last place five seasons in a row and were odds-on favorites to do it again. If playing these bums didn't break Babe Ruth and the Yankees out of their slump, I didn't know what would.

The only thing interesting about the current edition of the A's was Connie Mack himself. He was in charge of everything from making trades, to signing players to contracts, to calling pitches. He never wore a uniform. I could see the old gentleman now, sitting tall on the visitors' bench, in a suit, necktie, and straw boater. He looked more like a farmer dressed up to ask for a loan at the bank than a baseball man.

Babe trotted onto the field, still tucking in his uniform shirt, as Jack Quinn, the Yankees starting pitcher, climbed onto the mound. The owners had passed a new rule outlawing the spitball. But each team was allowed to name one player who depended on the trick pitch. That individual would be allowed to slobber on the ball for the rest of his career. Quinn chewed slimy tobacco that he used to grease the baseball. When his pitches broke, the A's were helpless. But, every once in a while, he threw a straight one that got hit hard.

Luckily, the Yankees had no problem with the A's starter, Rollie Naylor, tattooing him for eight runs. Babe didn't hit a homer, but he smacked two doubles off the wall in right center field.

I enjoyed watching Connie Mack. He held a score-card in his hands and waved it back and forth to position his fielders before every batter. It seemed to me that he was wrong as often as he was right. But you could see that if a fellow wanted to play for Philadelphia, he had to do what Mr. Mack said. I guess it's easy to get folks to listen if you own the team. The Yankees didn't operate that way. Players turned and walked away from Miller Huggins as if he were an annoying insect.

Babe was all smiles after the victory. "You brought me luck, Kid," he said. "Tomorrow's an off day. Can you throw a few more?"

"Sure, Babe. I'll be here."

"Practice ends at noon. I'll take a few extra swings, then we'll find that hot dog wagon again." He smacked me on the back and headed for the showers.

Ten minutes later we were leaning against the hot dog wagon while the owner buried our dogs in sauerkraut. "These are the best, Babe," I said, taking my first bite.

Babe froze, his hot dog dangling tantalizingly in front of his lips. "Naw. These are good, but nothing beats a Coney Island dog."

"What's so great about them?"

"You mean you're what . . . fifteen, sixteen, and you never had a Coney?"

I nodded. I'd heard of Coney Island, of course. Who hadn't? I knew it was in Brooklyn, not far from Ebbets Field. Folks said there was a park filled with rides and car- nival booths right next to the ocean.

"Let's fix that right now," Babe said. He bit off half a hot dog and started down the block. I didn't know if I was keeping my promise to Huggins or breaking it, but I hus- tled to catch up.

"It's ten miles or more to Brooklyn," I complained. "How long will it take to get there?"

"We'll ride a subway, Kid. It don't matter how many horses and wagons clog the streets. There's always an open road down there."

When we got to the station, Babe forked over a couple nickels, and we boarded the train. "It smells brand new," I said.

"Those hot dogs with kraut we just ate will change that fast enough," Babe said with a belch.

The car left the platform and dipped underground. The sudden darkness made me nervous. It didn't seem to be roaring along under the earth with all those

Wild Ride

B ill Pennant was behaving more like a wild animal every day. He seemed to spend most of his time hiding out in the travel crate. When I approached the cage, he'd commence to snarling. Didn't he know I was there to feed him?

John McGraw would be back in town in a few days. The next stop on the road trip was Ebbets Field in Brooklyn. The Giants would live at home and ride the train to the games. I'd have to tell Mr. McGraw there was no way his plan was going to work. If Bill Pennant had ever been trainable, the time had passed.

Today Billy's hunger must have had an edge. The moment I slid his dish into the cage, he burst out of his travel box, leaving a tuft of fur hanging from its doorway. I yanked my hand back so quickly that I scraped myself on the wire. While I sucked the pain out of my hand, Bill leaped at the sardines.

I hadn't seen him up close in a while, and it took me a moment to realize what was different. Bill Pennant took up a lot more space than he used to. His paws didn't look so out of proportion with his new barrel-chested body. Suddenly, Billy stopped eating and stared at me. His eyes were so penetrating that I took a step back. He strutted over to the barrier that separated us and, without taking his eyes from mine, licked my blood from the wire. That gave me such a crawly feeling that it raised the goose flesh on my arms. I headed for the locker room.

It was strange to open my locker and find two uniforms. The Giants and the Yankees were in opposite leagues, played opposite styles of baseball, and had managers who couldn't have been more different from each other. They shared just two things—the Polo Grounds and me.

Babe was late for practice. I thought I'd shag some flies and help out wherever an extra pair of hands was needed. But when I ran out to left field, Carl Mays pointed at me and said, "Scram."

I kept moving, figuring I'd give right field a try. "Hey, you," Mays hollered. I looked over my shoulder at him. "Off the field. No kids allowed."

I didn't move, so he started toward me. What made Carl Mays so special? If Babe Ruth wanted me around, that should be good enough for any of the Yankees. Mays and I were standing, jaw to jaw, when Huggins called me. I loped toward the dugout.

74

"Carl's pitching tomorrow," Huggins said. "He's t[…] as a drum the day before. Stay away from him."

If it were me, I'd wonder what my pitcher had to[…] nervous about. But I took Huggins's advice and kep[…] straightening the bats. You could pick out the Babe['s?…] a distance. No one else swung a club anywhere n[…] size of his.

It was another half-hour before Babe showed[…] strolled into the dugout, winked at me, and gra[…] bat. He pushed in front of a rookie, who had b[…] ing for a chance to hit, and hopped into the ba[…] McGraw would have been all over him. Hugg[…] relieved that he was there.

When he was done hitting, Babe flop[…] bench. "Is something wrong?" Huggins asked[…]

"Naw, Skip. My ankle's a little sore. D[…] make it worse chasing fly balls. I'll rest it tod[…] for the game tomorrow."

Huggins sighed and turned away. Babe[…] and sprayed a stream of tobacco juice on[…] manager's socks and shoes. A couple of t[…] out laughing. They stopped when Hug[…] with a glare. By the time he looked at[…] lowered his cap over his eyes and was pr[…]

Babe lazed on the bench for the re[…] When practice ended, Roger Peckinpa[…] that landed in Babe's lap. He didn't s[…] players and manager had left, and[…] equipment, did Babe stretch, yawn[…] hungry, Kid?"

75

Wild
Ride

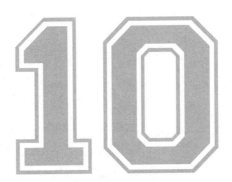

B ill Pennant was behaving more like a wild animal every day. He seemed to spend most of his time hiding out in the travel crate. When I approached the cage, he'd commence to snarling. Didn't he know I was there to feed him?

John McGraw would be back in town in a few days. The next stop on the road trip was Ebbets Field in Brooklyn. The Giants would live at home and ride the train to the games. I'd have to tell Mr. McGraw there was no way his plan was going to work. If Bill Pennant had ever been trainable, the time had passed.

Today Billy's hunger must have had an edge. The moment I slid his dish into the cage, he burst out of his travel box, leaving a tuft of fur hanging from its doorway. I yanked my hand back so quickly that I scraped myself on the wire. While I sucked the pain out of my hand, Bill leaped at the sardines.

I hadn't seen him up close in a while, and it took me a moment to realize what was different. Bill Pennant took up a lot more space than he used to. His paws didn't look so out of proportion with his new barrel-chested body. Suddenly, Billy stopped eating and stared at me. His eyes were so penetrating that I took a step back. He strutted over to the barrier that separated us and, without taking his eyes from mine, licked my blood from the wire. That gave me such a crawly feeling that it raised the goose flesh on my arms. I headed for the locker room.

It was strange to open my locker and find two uniforms. The Giants and the Yankees were in opposite leagues, played opposite styles of baseball, and had managers who couldn't have been more different from each other. They shared just two things—the Polo Grounds and me.

Babe was late for practice. I thought I'd shag some flies and help out wherever an extra pair of hands was needed. But when I ran out to left field, Carl Mays pointed at me and said, "Scram."

I kept moving, figuring I'd give right field a try. "Hey, you," Mays hollered. I looked over my shoulder at him. "Off the field. No kids allowed."

I didn't move, so he started toward me. What made Carl Mays so special? If Babe Ruth wanted me around, that should be good enough for any of the Yankees. Mays and I were standing, jaw to jaw, when Huggins called me. I loped toward the dugout.

"Carl's pitching tomorrow," Huggins said. "He's tight as a drum the day before. Stay away from him."

If it were me, I'd wonder what my pitcher had to be so nervous about. But I took Huggins's advice and kept busy straightening the bats. You could pick out the Babe's from a distance. No one else swung a club anywhere near the size of his.

It was another half-hour before Babe showed up. He strolled into the dugout, winked at me, and grabbed his bat. He pushed in front of a rookie, who had been waiting for a chance to hit, and hopped into the batter's box. McGraw would have been all over him. Huggins looked relieved that he was there.

When he was done hitting, Babe flopped on the bench. "Is something wrong?" Huggins asked.

"Naw, Skip. My ankle's a little sore. Don't want to make it worse chasing fly balls. I'll rest it today and be fine for the game tomorrow."

Huggins sighed and turned away. Babe winked at me and sprayed a stream of tobacco juice on the back of the manager's socks and shoes. A couple of the rookies burst out laughing. They stopped when Huggins fixed them with a glare. By the time he looked at Ruth, Babe had lowered his cap over his eyes and was pretending to sleep.

Babe lazed on the bench for the rest of the workout. When practice ended, Roger Peckinpaugh lobbed a towel that landed in Babe's lap. He didn't stir. Only when the players and manager had left, and I was done storing equipment, did Babe stretch, yawn, and say, "Are you hungry, Kid?"

Ten minutes later we were leaning against the hot dog wagon while the owner buried our dogs in sauerkraut. "These are the best, Babe," I said, taking my first bite.

Babe froze, his hot dog dangling tantalizingly in front of his lips. "Naw. These are good, but nothing beats a Coney Island dog."

"What's so great about them?"

"You mean you're what . . . fifteen, sixteen, and you never had a Coney?"

I nodded. I'd heard of Coney Island, of course. Who hadn't? I knew it was in Brooklyn, not far from Ebbets Field. Folks said there was a park filled with rides and carnival booths right next to the ocean.

"Let's fix that right now," Babe said. He bit off half a hot dog and started down the block. I didn't know if I was keeping my promise to Huggins or breaking it, but I hustled to catch up.

"It's ten miles or more to Brooklyn," I complained. "How long will it take to get there?"

"We'll ride a subway, Kid. It don't matter how many horses and wagons clog the streets. There's always an open road down there."

When we got to the station, Babe forked over a couple of nickels, and we boarded the train. "It smells brand new," I said.

"Those hot dogs with kraut we just ate will change that fast enough," Babe said with a belch.

The car left the platform and dipped underground. The sudden darkness made me nervous. It didn't seem safe to be roaring along under the earth with all those heavy buildings pushing down on us, so I tried to get a conversation going. "Who's the best player in the league, Babe?"

"You're sitting next to him, Kid. Who else can strike out the best hitters and knock out the best pitchers?"

"Besides you. What about Cobb?"

"Cobb's over the hill. His game is dead. Why bunt and run the bases in a panic when you can hit the ball over the wall and stroll at your own pace? It's more manly."

"I named myself after Cobb. My old man said he was the best ever."

"Was," Babe said, poking a finger into my ribs. "Maybe Cobb was the best, but not anymore."

A few minutes later, we piled up a flight of steps into the April sunshine. I had expected Coney Island to be a hubbub, but the street was empty. Babe looked puzzled, too. "It wasn't like this when I visited with some of the Red Sox. Everyone was having a high old time," he said.

We crossed the Bowery and headed down the street. I could see all kinds of rides in the distance, but it didn't look like any of them were running. We passed carnival booths, their brightly colored signs offering popcorn, candy, and the hot dogs we had come for. Problem was, padlocked sheets of wood covered their windows.

Babe pointed at an arched wooden gateway with a bright yellow clown's face hanging from its center. "Steeplechase. That's where the best rides are. We'll go on the roller coaster, then pound some hot dogs."

That sequence made sense to me. I had never been on a coaster, but the fellows at school said they could make you sick to your stomach. No way did I want to see the Babe unload hot dogs and sauerkraut. We passed through the gate and walked down another lifeless street. "I don't think the park is open, Babe," I said.

If he heard me, it only made him more determined. A hammering noise started up. Babe strode toward it, with me hoofing behind him. When we found the work crew, they were admiring a sign they had just hung in front of a mountain of wooden boards that looked like it had been cobbled together by a madman. The sign said Drop the Dip.

"There it is, Kid," Babe said, his grin nearly matching the Steeplechase clown's. "Fastest coaster on Coney Island."

It was tall, maybe five or six stories. But how fast could a ride be that looked like it was made from over-sized matchsticks? Babe went to talk to the workmen. I moved closer to Drop the Dip.

I walked along a wooden sidewalk, gawking like a rube. Within the confused tangle of supports, I made out the underside of a train track that ran up and down hills and twisted and turned its way along the beach.

When I reached the far end, I used Damon Runyon's trick and counted how many strides it took me to rejoin Babe and the workmen. I counted two hundred of my steps. My stride was shorter than Runyon's, maybe two and a half feet instead of three. I estimated that the ride was about five hundred feet long.

Babe was talking and waving his arms. The others

shook their heads. I couldn't make out all their words with the shore breezes whipping. I got the gist of it, though. Steeplechase and the two other amusement parks at Coney Island didn't open for another week.

Babe reached into a jacket pocket and pulled out a flask. He took a long pull, then passed it around the circle of men. By the time the container was empty, they had their arms around each other and were laughing like old buddies. Babe waved for me to come over.

"Kid, we've got an important job to do. We're going to help these fellows out by testing their roller coaster. We'll make sure it's safe for the public to ride."

Suddenly that heap of boards looked twice as tall. I searched for an excuse. "You're not scared, are you, Kid?" Babe asked.

That got me moving. Girls went on these rides. There wasn't anything in Coney Island that could frighten me. I walked alongside Babe as one of the crew unlocked a chain barrier and lowered it to the ground. He took a canvas cover off a clump of machinery, tinkered for a moment, then jumped back as a motor roared to life with an ungodly cough and whine. Black smoke swept over us, but Babe just laughed.

"Don't worry, Kid. It's clearing its throat after a long winter. Sounds a little like me when I wake up in the morning."

There was a line of cars, each one made to look like some fancy kind of sled. Babe led the way to the first, and we climbed into the front seat. The man who had started the engine came over. He lowered an iron bar that pinned us against the seat back.

"This will keep you from flying out on the turns. Only ride in the world so fast that it needs a safety bar."

He rapped the side of our car with his knuckles, then scrambled back to the machinery. The engine noise had smoothed out a bit, and when he threw a big lever, our car started to move, pulling the other cars behind it.

We inched our way to the bottom of a steep hill. The track went up at such an angle that it was hard to believe the engine would have the power to get us to the top. A clunking noise made me look over the side in case the track was breaking. Then we started up. Every few seconds there was another clunk. I realized that each time we gained a few feet, something locked behind us to keep us from rolling back.

We finally reached the peak. The track curved sharply downward, and I could see the ocean in the distance. Babe pulled off his cap and stuck it under his belt. "If you've got any loose teeth, Kid, keep your mouth closed," he teased.

Before I could think of a smart remark to throw back at him, I heard a final clunk. This one released us, and the car hurtled downward. My skin stretched across my face as if someone had grabbed my ears and was trying to tie them in a knot behind my head.

We plowed into a curve that threw Babe Ruth's weight against me so that I could barely breathe. Just when I thought I couldn't stand it, the car leaned toward Babe, and I slammed against his side.

The next hill was less steep, but the curves were even sharper. For a split second, I was sure we would hurtle off the tracks, into the blue sky, to crash on the beach. But we made it, wheels groaning in protest, as Babe smooshed me again.

That coaster pulled all its tricks three times before we eased to a stop at the boarding area. The operator lifted the safety bar. Babe and I climbed out, staggering dizzily, smiles plastered on our mugs. "That gave me an appetite," Babe said. "Where can we get a couple of Nathan's finest?"

Following the operator's directions, we walked a block inland to a joint that was open year round. It was doing a steady business feeding the workers who were getting Coney Island's rides and attractions in shape for the new season.

Babe ordered four dogs with everything, and I had to admit, they were better than the ones sold near the Polo Grounds. I polished off one and was too full to even think about the other. It didn't go to waste. Babe finished it in three bites.

"Well, Kid, let's catch the subway to Manhattan," Babe said, wiping mustard from his face with his sleeve.

"Too late," said the counterman. "Last train of the day left ten minutes ago. Reduced schedule during the off-season."

Babe thumped the counter with his fist. "I can't spend the night in Brooklyn. There's a dame waiting for me."

Wilder Ride

I didn't want to spend the night in Brooklyn, either. How would I explain that to Mrs. McGraw? Plus, I owed Billy a meal. I'd hate to ruin his sunny disposition by letting him go to bed hungry.

Babe pulled a wad of cash from his pocket, waved it in the air, and called, "Who can give us a ride to Manhattan?"

The workmen looked at each other. A small man in a suit pushed himself out of a booth and walked toward us. He slid onto the stool next to Babe and stuck out his hand. "John Finney."

The Babe shook hands and said, "Are you going to take us home?"

"Better than that, Mr. . . . . ?"

Babe took off his cap. "Don't you know who I am? Tell him, Kid."

I didn't miss my cue. "This is Babe Ruth, home run champion of the major leagues, star outfielder of the New York Yankees, World Series record-setting pitcher. Why, he batted—"

Babe clamped a hand on my wrist. "He gets the idea, Kid."

"Babe Ruth, eh?" Finney said. "Well, Mr. Ruth, a man of your status doesn't belong on public transportation. You should have your own automobile."

"I had one in Boston, a flivver. Damn thing kept breaking down, so I left it there when I got sold to the Yankees."

"That's because you didn't buy the best." Finney leaned past Babe and looked at me. "What's the finest automobile on the market, young man?"

That was an easy one. I had seen plenty of ads in those fancy magazines the McGraws subscribed to. "Locomobile," I answered.

"The Locomobile, indeed," Finney said, nodding his head in agreement. "Mr. Ruth, you are speaking to Brooklyn's only authorized Locomobile dealer. How would you like to climb behind the wheel of the finest machine on the road today?"

"What do you take me for, some kind of sucker?" Babe asked, fists clenching and cheeks puffing out. "The Locomobile is custom order. I'd be lucky to have it in time for the World Series. How is that going to get me to Manhattan tonight?"

"Calm yourself, Mr. Ruth. It happens that I took delivery yesterday for a customer, and he was . . . unavoidably . . . unable to accept his purchase."

"The cops hauled him off to jail," explained the counterman as he wiped up relish that had flown from one of Babe's hot dogs.

"Quite," said Mr. Finney. "So, I've got this beautiful machine, and you, sir, are obviously the type of man who demands the finest."

"How much?" Babe asked.

"Don't you want to hear about the luxury features? The engine is so quiet that a small light on the dashboard alerts you when it's running."

"How much?"

"Twelve thousand dollars."

"Twelve thousand? I can get a Model T for six hundred."

"Got one myself," interrupted the counterman. "Runs like a top."

"What would your fans think if they saw the mighty Babe Ruth driving a car that any one of them could own? They might wonder if you were really such a unique athlete after all."

"Especially when you haven't hit a single home run this season," said the counterman.

Babe pulled rumpled wads of money from each of his front pockets and threw them on the counter. "How about three hundred dollars for a down payment? Come to the Polo Grounds tomorrow. If I like the car, I'll give you the rest of the money. If not, you can keep one hundred dollars."

"Make my guarantee two hundred, and you've got a deal," Finney said.

"Count that money for me, Kid. See what I've got."

My hands were shaking. I smoothed out the bills one by one, keeping a close eye on the counterman in case he tried to sweep any over the edge with that rag of his. Babe was walking around with $537 jammed in his pockets. No wonder he never minded paying for our hot dogs.

I separated three hundred dollars, and Babe passed it to Finney. The rest he crammed into his pants, except for a five-dollar bill he left for the counterman. "Where's my car?" was Babe's only question.

It turned out that Finney's Finest, Brooklyn's Elite Automobile Supplier, was a short walk from the hot dog stand. The Locomobile was in back of the dealership, under a canvas tarp. At first glance, it looked as big as some of the rides at Coney Island.

"Congratulations, Mr. Ruth," Finney said. "Behold the 1920 Locomobile." He unhooked the tarp and swept it away. The Locomobile was silver with chrome trim that sparkled in the late afternoon sun. Babe gave one of the tires a kick. Then he put both hands on the front fender and rocked the car up and down.

Finney shuddered, using a snot-rag to rub away Babe's finger marks. He spat on one corner, but before he could wash Babe's toe print off the white-sidewall tire, Babe said, "Let's have the keys. We're running late."

"Come inside first. There are papers to sign."

"Go get the papers while I warm up the engine," Babe insisted.

"The keys are inside as well," Finney said. Babe didn't budge. Finney went for the keys.

I was walking around and around the car, hardly able to believe my eyes. "Are you really going to buy it, Babe?"

He winked at me. "Nah. What would I do with a fancy boat like this? We'll use it to get home tonight, and Finney can drive it back here tomorrow."

"What about the money?"

Babe shrugged. "He'll give most of it back. Who's going to give Babe Ruth a hard time at the Polo Grounds?"

I wanted to say what a bad idea I thought all this was, but Finney was returning, a set of keys in one hand and a bundle of papers in the other. "Now, if I could point out some of the features—," he began.

"Just point me toward Manhattan and get out of the way," Babe said. "Where do I sign?"

"Don't you want to read the contract first?"

"I trust you. Cheat Babe Ruth and half the people in New York will come after you. It'd wreck your business."

Finney sighed and leafed through the packet of papers. He pointed to a line and handed Babe a fountain pen and the contract. Babe set the paper on the hood of the Locomobile and scrawled *George Ruth*, his tongue sticking out of the corner of his mouth as he formed the letters. "Keys," he demanded.

Finney reluctantly handed Babe the keys. "Where do we meet tomorrow?"

"Be at the players' entrance at one-thirty. Is cash all right?" Babe asked.

The thought of collecting twelve thousand dollars in cash seemed to remove Finney's last doubts. He gave Babe directions to the Brooklyn Bridge. Once we had crossed, we would be in Manhattan. We climbed into the car, me feeling lost on the huge front seat.

A crystal container was mounted on the inside of each door. "Look, Kid, built-in spittoons," Babe said. He shot a stream of tobacco juice that oozed down the inside of the one on the driver's door.

"Actually, those are bud vases," Finney said. I'm not sure Babe heard. He tipped his cap and eased the big boat onto the street.

The dashboard had so many gauges that if the driver tried to read them all, he would never get a chance to look at the road. Even the gearshift was fancy. Babe wrapped his hand over a gold knob that looked like the handle of an expensive walking stick.

"Well, Kid, let's see what she can do," Babe said and stomped the gas pedal to the floor. I thought I was back on Drop the Dip, this time without a safety bar. The Locomobile gained speed at a frightening rate. Babe spun the steering wheel between his hands, leaving it to faith that there wouldn't be anything or anyone in our way when we rounded a curve. I flopped around on the leather seat, sliding back and forth, until I got a death grip on the door handle.

By the time I spotted the turn for the Brooklyn Bridge, Babe was almost past it. He whipped the wheel to the right, tires screaming. We held the road somehow and sped up the ramp. At the top, there was a big hole in the pavement. Babe tried to straddle it, but the right front wheel slammed to the bottom. I flew off the seat as that one wheel stopped and the rest of the car kept moving. My head rammed the ceiling, and I remember thinking that it was not nearly as soft and cushiony as it looked.

The Locomobile spun and came to a stop facing back down the ramp. A ramshackle truck was coming toward us. I could see the driver's eyes getting bigger as he stood on his brakes. Babe's sigh matched mine when the truck came to a halt, inches from the Locomobile's gleaming chrome bumper.

Hiding the Evidence 12

I t took another chunk of the cash that Babe was carrying, but the trucker agreed to tow us into the city. I had an egg on top of my head where I had whanged it on the ceiling. Babe rubbed his right knee, but wouldn't admit there was anything wrong with it. We sat crammed in the cab of the truck, people gawking at the magnificent, three-wheeled car limping along behind us.

The trucker dropped me at the Polo Grounds before driving on to find a mechanic for the Locomobile. I fed Bill Pennant, an occasional hiss from the travel crate his only sign of interest. Since it was getting dark, I left the American Flyer in the locker room and walked the two miles to Graham Court.

The second I caught sight of the McGraws' apartment,

I knew I was in trouble. Every light was blazing. The night doorman, a nervous sort named Ralph, let me in, inspecting me from head to toe to make sure I was in one piece. I had my cap on, so he didn't notice the knot on my skull. Ralph said, "Get up there, quick, before Mrs. McGraw has the police after you."

I hustled up the grand staircase and opened the apartment door. Mrs. McGraw came to meet me. "You're alive, then."

"I'm fine."

"Do you know how many boys end up in the hospital from cycling in the dark?"

"I walked home."

"Do you know how many boys have been flattened by trucks, walking the city in the dark?"

"I stayed on the sidewalk."

"How would I explain to Mr. McGraw if something happened to you the first day he was away? What were you doing all this time? You can't play baseball at night."

This took some thinking. I didn't want to lie, but I couldn't very well say that I had ridden a roller coaster at Coney Island and been in a car accident on the Brooklyn Bridge. "Miller Huggins asked me to spend some time with Babe Ruth, keep him out of trouble."

"Babe Ruth?" I nodded. "You'll not keep his hours and live here. I want you home before dark from now on."

"I promise," I said, thinking that would be the end of it.

Mrs. McGraw walked away shaking her head. Halfway down the hall she turned. "You do know that Mr. McGraw has no use for the man?"

I nodded again, and this time she left me in peace.

My dreams were filled with twisting roller coasters and screeching brakes. I was more tired in the morning than I had been at bedtime. I usually don't fuss with my hair other than to spit in my palms and glue down any clumps that are sticking up. But this morning I went into John McGraw's bathroom to borrow some of the bear grease that he used. I wasn't turning into a fancy boy. I wanted to conceal the lump the Locomobile's ceiling had raised on my skull. Last night I had hidden it under my cap, but I knew Mrs. McGraw wouldn't let me sit at the breakfast table with my head covered.

John McGraw was a rough character. But if you hadn't met him, and looked into his bathroom, you wouldn't think so. His shelf held a half-dozen bottles of hair tonic, each more fragrant than the last. I chose a brand called Petrole. It was the only one that didn't make my eyes water when I whiffed it.

I rubbed a gob into the shock of hair that hung over my forehead and pulled it straight back in a pile that covered the lump. That stuff was better than glue. The bottle promised that it would prevent unsightly dandruff flakes, and I'll bet it worked. If the dandruff was glued to your scalp, it couldn't fall off and cover your shoulders.

Mrs. McGraw raised her eyebrows when she saw me. "Combing your hair? Is that Babe Ruth's influence?"

I could feel my cheeks turning red. "It was hanging in my eyes."

"There's a barbershop down the street."

"I like it this way," I said, dishing myself some oatmeal.

91

"I guess you're entitled after what you went through last season." I didn't like being reminded of my days running around with a shaven head to bring the Giants luck, but at least it got Mrs. McGraw to stop plaguing me.

Once she picked up the newspaper, I was free to shovel in the food. Within minutes, I had excused myself, dumped my bowl in the sink, and left the apartment. The walk to the Polo Grounds seemed long now that I had been spoiled by riding the American Flyer. But if things worked out, I'd be back in the saddle for the trip home.

Bill Pennant hid until I had filled his dish and relocked the cage. I clomped down the hall, making as much noise as possible, then tiptoed back to watch. Billy slunk from the travel crate and climbed the tree branch. He lay motionless for a minute, then pounced on the dish of food, scattering sardines all over the cage. I shook my head and went into the locker room to put on my uniform.

Most of the Yankees were dressed, and there was no sign of Babe Ruth. I started to get nervous that he wouldn't show up at the ballpark before Finney. I didn't want to be called on to explain what had happened to the Locomobile.

Ping Bodie, the center fielder and Babe's roommate on road trips, was pulling on his stirrups. "Have you seen the Babe?" I asked.

"I know where he is, if that's what you want to know."

I waited, but he made me ask. "Where is he?"

"He and Huggins are in Colonel Ruppert's office."

That was bad. Jacob Ruppert was the team's owner. He lived outside the city, in a mansion along the Hudson River. For him to be at the ballpark this early on a weekday, something was wrong. He sure wasn't here to watch the A's.

Thirty minutes before game time, Babe walked in. He must have been chewed out pretty good, because he went straight to his locker and started to dress. By the time I got close enough to ask him what had happened, he was lacing up his spikes.

"When I took the car in for repairs, some fool mechanic called Finney to ask a question about it. His name and number must have been on the owner's manual. Finney telephoned the Colonel without even giving me a chance to pay him his money."

"Do you have to buy the car?"

"Lucky for me, the Colonel wants it. Says a ballplayer has no business driving a Locomobile." Babe waved his hands as if to erase what he had said. "That's not why he's mad. Ruppert's steamed about the team's slow start. Like everyone else in New York, he blames me for not hitting any home runs yet."

Babe limped onto the field. I hoped his sore knee would hold out. If the accident knocked him from the lineup, he'd be in more trouble. Huggins came in a minute later, glaring at me as if I had let him down. If he and the Colonel couldn't control Babe Ruth, I don't know how they expected me to. I made myself useful hauling water to the dugout.

The Polo Grounds was about half full, a good crowd for this early in the season. Carl Mays was pitching for the Yankees. Part of me wanted to see him get roughed up for being so nasty. But I planned to root for him, since I wanted the Yankees to win. I always studied a pitcher to try and see how he got batters out. Watching Carl Mays warm up, he almost had me laughing. His arms flew over his head like one of those old-timey pitchers the old man used to talk about. Then he dipped so low that his knuckles nearly scraped the ground before he let go of the ball. He pitched so differently from anyone I had ever seen, that I couldn't figure out how he could be effective.

Then the game started. The A's had lots of right-handed hitters, and they looked like they would rather pull their own teeth with a rusty pair of pliers than stand in the batter's box against Mays. He stepped toward third base as he wound up. When he released the ball from ground level, it zoomed up at the batter, barely squeezing past him to cross the plate.

If you had told me I would be scared to stand in against a pitcher, I would have laughed—until I saw Carl Mays. Something about his underhand motion made it hard to judge the speed of the ball. You wanted to hang in and watch for a curve, but if you guessed wrong, the ball would be in your face before you could get out of the way.

The Athletics scored two runs, one on an error, and the other when Mays drilled a batter in the ribs with the bases loaded. The Yankees made three, two coming home on a Babe Ruth double. It was harder than it should have been, but the team had its second win in a row. After the game, Babe cleared out before I had a chance to talk to him. I fed Billy and rode home on the Flyer, making it before sunset.

Mrs. McGraw was out, but she had left a key with the doorman and a sandwich in the icebox. I spent the evening reading the papers and trying not to think about batting against Carl Mays. The Giants had been rained out for a second day in a row in Boston. After today's game, they were heading home to play the Robins in Brooklyn. That meant John McGraw would be here when I got up in the morning. I wondered how he would take it when I told him that I was getting nowhere with Bill Pennant.

An article in the *New York Sun* gave me something else to worry about. "Ruth in Crash," the headline read. *Babe Ruth and an unidentified passenger narrowly escaped serious injury last night when their car ran off the entrance ramp to the Brooklyn Bridge. Ruth was driving a 1920 Locomobile valued at $12,000.* I could imagine John McGraw's reaction if he ever found out I was in that car with the Babe.

McGraw was seated at the table, face hidden by a newspaper, when I came to breakfast. Mrs. McGraw warned me of his mood by picking up her teacup and retreating to her bedroom. "Thanks for the bicycle. It's great," I said.

McGraw grunted, so I tried another slant. "How'd the team do yesterday?"

He folded the newspaper and set it on the table. His eyes blazed. "Which team are you interested in, the Giants or the Yankees?"

My throat was tight. "I know the Yankees won. I was at the game."

"Do you think I'm paying your salary so you can root for a big ape who's ruining the game of baseball?"

I know it was wrong, but my temper flared. "I do my job. Billy's fat and sassy."

"How much time have you spent with him? Is he ready to be seen by the public without running wild?"

"I don't think anyone can train that cat. It's all I can do to feed him and clean up his messes without losing an arm."

McGraw sighed. "He hasn't brought us any luck. Yesterday was the first game we played without Bill Pennant in the ballpark, and we scored seven runs. It took us a week to get that many at the Polo Grounds."

McGraw pushed his chair back from the table, got up, and paced the kitchen the same way he strode the dugout in a tight game, beating the folded newspaper against his leg with each step. "I'm starting to think that cat is a jinx. Maybe I should get rid of him."

"Would that mean I could travel with the team again?" I couldn't help but ask.

"No, Hank. It means you could go back to school where you belong. God knows what you've been learning from Babe Ruth."

"I don't need schooling. Baseball's my trade. Besides, you said you needed me."

Hiding the Evidence

"And you said you were a Giant!" McGraw slammed the newspaper on the table, spilling what was left of his coffee. He stomped out of the room, leaving me to stare at a photograph of myself standing next to Babe Ruth, both of us in pinstripes.

Caught
Stealing

I took off for the Polo Grounds without finishing breakfast. The Sunday morning streets were quiet, and it should have been a pleasure to cruise along on the American Flyer. But the cycle made me think of John McGraw, and I couldn't think of him without being angry. I longed to travel the country in style, like I had last year, moving from ballpark to ballpark with nothing to worry about except helping the team to win. Instead I was stuck in New York, nursemaid to a jinx. Split between two teams, it didn't feel like I was any use to either of them.

My mind was set on one thing. I wasn't going back to school—not ever. If McGraw didn't want me, I'd ask Huggins to put me on the Yankee payroll. Even if it meant returning my beautiful cycle and finding a new place to live.

Caught Stealing

The weather was as nasty as my mood. It was one of those April days where you have to keep telling yourself that winter is over. A cold wind stung my face, and it felt as if it might start raining at any moment.

By the time I got to the Polo Grounds, I was shivering. After feeding a sullen Bill Pennant, I pulled on my uniform. I was still cold. I wanted to wear a heavy sweater like the players did on chilly, damp days. Problem was, the only sweater I had was from the Giants.

Winning a ball game hadn't improved Carl Mays's mood. He glared at me when he came into the locker room, and I made myself scarce. I grabbed a broom and swept the dugout, making the job last until the players came out to warm up.

Babe was on time for once, probably because of the bawling out he'd received the day before. I watched him take batting practice, and his sore right knee buckled a couple of times. I rubbed the lump on my head. It had gotten a lot smaller, but neither one of us was at full strength yet.

By game time, an icy rain was falling, and fewer than a thousand bugs filled the seats. Rollie Naylor was on the mound for the Athletics for the second time in the series. Today, the Yankees couldn't hit him. Bob Shawkey started for the home team. He didn't give up a run until the seventh inning when the A's scored twice.

The game was decided in the Yankees' half of the seventh. Babe knocked in a run with a single and was on first base with two men out. The situation called for caution, yet Babe took off for second, bad knee and all, on the first pitch to Ping Bodie. He should have been out by a mile, but Cy Perkins, the A's catcher, was so surprised to see Babe running that he was slow to react.

Cy's throw was strong, arriving at second base the same time as Ruth. Babe waited too long to slide and was moving too fast when he reached the bag. His foot stopped, but the rest of his leg kept moving, twisting into an unnatural shape. When he rolled off the bag in pain, second baseman Jimmy Dykes slapped the tag on him for the third out. No Yankee was allowed to steal without a sign from the manager. When I saw Huggins kick his own hat across the dugout, I knew Babe had broken that rule.

While the A's ran off the field, Babe writhed on the ground, gripping the knee he had banged in the car wreck. Believe it or not, he called me. "Hey, Kid, bring me a ball bat. Maybe I can pound this knee into place."

I ran for the dugout, but when I got there, Huggins motioned me to sit down and trotted onto the field. Carl Mays said, "I'd run his bat out there, but I'm liable to beat the big dummy over the head with it. Since when did he become a base stealer?"

Huggins crouched and felt Babe's knee. He yelled, "Meusel, French," and the two rookies nearly tripped each other scrambling up the steps. When they reached second, they lifted Babe to his feet. He hopped off the field, one arm around each man's shoulders, his damaged leg dangling in the air.

There weren't many bugs left in the stands, but those who had stayed weren't bashful about expressing their opinion of Babe's performance. They stood as one and booed. A car took Babe to a hospital named Columbia-Perspiration, or something like that. His teammates went quietly in the last two innings, losing to the pathetic A's by a score of two to one.

Afterwards, no one spoke in the locker room. The players communicated by slamming lockers and kicking benches. As soon as Billy was fed, I left.

I was moping around the Graham Court apartment, when I heard a key in the door. I braced myself for more of John McGraw's anger, but the man who entered, arm in arm with his missus, was all smiles. "You should have seen it, Hank. We taught those Robins a lesson today."

"That's great, Mr. McGraw."

"How did the Yankees do?"

"They lost two to one." I didn't mention Babe's injury. If he acted happy about that, it would only make me sore.

"A good day all around," McGraw said with a smile. "Maybe Bill Pennant is putting the whammy on them."

"None of the Yankees go near him," I said.

"I'd sure like to find a new home for him before May 5. I don't want Bill Pennant messing up our next home game."

I lay in my bed that night and wondered how much longer Bill Pennant would be with the team. And when Bill left, would I be leaving, too? The threat of school kept me squirming until the sheets were in knots.

 Keeping
Score

I awoke to the sound of rain drumming against my bedroom window. One look at the sky, and I knew there wouldn't be a ball game at the Polo Grounds today, and probably not in Brooklyn, either. I would have gone back to sleep, but I had to take care of Billy.

John McGraw was at the breakfast table working his way through a pot of coffee and a stack of newspapers. "I see your boy has made more trouble for himself," he said, passing me the sports page.

The headline read, "Ruth Faces Fine and Suspension," and had Damon Runyon's byline. *George Herman Ruth has larceny in his heart. Unfortunately for the New York Yankees, his feet are honest.*

Leave it to Runyon to lead with a joke. The story

went on to say that Huggins planned to ask owner Jacob Ruppert to suspend Babe for running without permission. The good news was that his knee was only strained. A few days on crutches, and he would be healed.

"Ruth is lucky it's raining," McGraw said when I set down the paper. "One less game he'll miss because of his own stupidity."

Babe shouldn't have run, but I felt sorry for him. Huggins was out of line. You couldn't let a player ignore you at practice, then act surprised when he did it during a game. I was glad I had an excuse to leave, before I got into an argument with McGraw. Hadn't he ever done something dumb? I hated to get my new cycle wet, but I couldn't face a two-mile walk in the rain.

At the ballpark, I grabbed a towel and wiped the Flyer dry. I was shaking with cold, having been splashed by every car and truck that had passed me along the way. The concrete stadium oozed dampness, and the locker room was so quiet it was spooky. When a moaning wail pierced the air, I nearly cut and ran. The hair on my arms lay back down when I realized the sound must be from Bill Pennant.

I tiptoed down the hallway, stopping when I was close enough to see into his cage. Billy was stretched out on the tree branch, head hanging. Every few seconds, he'd let loose with the moaning cry. I don't know why Billy hated the cold and damp so much, but I knew why I did.

I'd lost my mother on a wintry night. It happened in a dingy room over a feed store in some little town in Iowa. We slept in our clothes, using our coats for blankets. My mother was burning with fever, so the old man and I lay on the floor.

He shook me awake in the morning, and I wanted to see how she was. The old man grabbed me by the belt and hustled me out of there. But I had seen the sheet pulled over her face, and I knew. I started wailing and couldn't stop. I thought the old man would leave me, too, but he tucked me under his arm and carried me. By the time we reached a railroad yard, I must have fallen asleep. Next thing I remember is opening my eyes to find I was rattling across the prairie in a boxcar.

As quietly as possible, I slid a fresh dish of food into Billy's cage. He didn't move, except for his eyes. They looked inside me and seemed to see the terrified little boy I thought I had left behind.

O'Hara brought me back to myself. "Will you give me a hand this morning, Hank?" he yelled from the end of the hall. I checked the lock on Billy's cage and went to see what he needed.

"This damp weather's warped the wooden scoreboard. The fellows had all they could do yesterday to fit the numbered tiles in their slots."

"What do you want me to do?" I asked.

"Put a coat of linseed oil on each one," he said, waving a metal can at me. "It will waterproof them and at the same time make them slick enough to slide easily."

I followed O'Hara out to left field. The rain had let up, but half the outfield was a pond. "Did you bring your rod and reel?" O'Hara joked.

He unlocked a door in the outfield wall with one of

his many keys. I went inside and wound up a flight of stairs in the half-light. At the top was a long, narrow room with two rows of small openings in one wall. I peered at the soggy field through the slot for the home team's first inning.

O'Hara set the can of linseed oil on the floor next to a beat-up chair. He pulled a rag from a jacket pocket and handed it to me. "In that bin," he pointed at a wooden crate underneath the rows of windows, "are the numbers used to show the score. Give each one a good coat, then spread them on the floor to dry. Damp as it is, it will take a while."

He started to leave, then turned and flipped me the key. "Lock up when you're through. Leave the key on top of your locker if I'm not around."

I got down to work. I decided it would be easiest to remove all the tiles first and dump them in a heap by the chair. When I dropped one bunch, I heard a clink that sounded more like metal than wood.

I crouched down and sifted through the pile. My fingers closed on a key. I held it against the key that O'Hara had left me, and it was a perfect match. I dropped them both into my pocket and got to work.

More tiles were marked zero than anything else, because most innings in baseball are scoreless. I started off polishing the zero tiles first, but after a while I just rubbed whatever I grabbed. By the time I was done, the can of oil was almost empty, and the floor was covered in shiny wooden tiles. There was just enough bare floor for me to tiptoe back to the staircase.

The rain had stopped, and the fresh air felt good after breathing the fumes from the oil in that closed space. The pond in the outfield had disappeared, but every step I took, water oozed up out of the ground. I wondered if the field would be ready to use tomorrow.

Not finding O'Hara, I stood on the bench to reach the top of my locker. When I dug in my pocket, I felt both keys. I don't know why, but I decided to keep the one I had found. I put the other right near the edge for O'Hara. Then I hopped down, left the oil and rag on the bench, and walked over to the American Flyer.

McGraw's voice stopped me in my tracks. "Is that you, Hank?"

I walked around to his office and found him sitting at his desk, a notebook open in front of him. "What are you doing here?" I asked.

"Trying to figure out a pitching rotation with all these rainouts." I noticed that everything written on the page had been crossed out.

"Making any progress?"

"None," he said, shoving back his chair. "Grab a bat and I'll throw you a few. I haven't seen you hit since last season."

McGraw didn't have to ask twice. This was my chance to show him the new Hank Cobb. No more bunts and half swings. Now I meant business when I stood at the plate.

I left a canvas sack of baseballs on the mound, set a hardly cracked bat George Burns had thrown away on the ground next to home plate, and pulled on an old catcher's mitt.

McGraw came out in uniform pants, a sweatshirt, and his oldest pair of cleats. In five minutes, his arm was loose, and I felt warm for the first time that day. "All right, Hank. Let's see what you can do."

I skidded the mitt toward the dugout, picked up the bat, and took my stance. McGraw went into his windup, then stopped. "Choke up," he yelled.

"I hold the bat at the end now," I explained. "Gives me more power."

"Power?" McGraw sneered. "You weigh a hundred twenty pounds. Choke up."

Smoke was coming out of my ears. "Throw the ball. Hitting it is my worry."

McGraw stared for a moment, then went into his windup. I swung with all my anger and missed a curve ball by a foot. The bat whacked me in the shoulder on my follow-through, but I tried to hide the pain.

"Nice swing, slugger," McGraw taunted.

I was steamed. In batting practice the pitcher is supposed to lay the ball in there, not throw breaking balls. I set myself for another curve, and a fast one zipped past me. "Strike!" McGraw shouted.

I managed to tip the next pitch as it dove into the dirt. "Throw strikes," I yelled.

"You look like a fool," McGraw said. "Smoky could fan you the way you're holding that bat. Have you forgotten everything I taught you last season?"

"Last season is over. This is how today's stars hit." I couldn't believe my own mouth.

McGraw didn't say another word. He threw me every type of pitch I had ever seen, and a few I hadn't heard about yet. I missed them all. It wasn't that he was extra fast or that his curves broke more than an average pitcher's. I just never knew what to expect. The more frustrated I got, the harder I swung. When I missed a change up so badly that I fell to the ground, I lost it completely.

I jumped up and threw the bat toward the stands. Without a word, I ran down the dugout steps, through the locker room, and out the players' entrance. I ran until I couldn't run another step, then ducked into an alley and sat with my head between my legs. John McGraw had humiliated me. He had to prove that he was right no matter how bad it made me feel. At that moment, I didn't want to ever see him again.

Interleague Trade

15

I moped around feeling sorry for myself until I was sure McGraw had left the ballpark. As I stood banging on the players' entrance, waiting for O'Hara to answer, the rain returned. I huddled against the building, the wind blowing the cold spray in my face, and started shivering again.

It finally occurred to me that O'Hara must have left for the day. I buried my hands in my pockets for warmth and felt the key I had found. Not expecting it to work, I slid it into the lock. I jiggled it back and forth and heard a click. For a moment I stood there, rain dripping from my cap down the back of my neck. Then I turned the doorknob and went inside.

I called O'Hara's name, debating whether I would own up to having the key, or try to convince him that the door had been unlocked. No one was around. I left food for an invisible Bill Pennant, then started to wheel my cycle toward the door. Instead, I lowered the stand and left it in the locker room. If I rode back to Graham Court, O'Hara would know I had been in the ballpark after he left. But, if I walked home, the key would be my secret. It felt good to have the key, good to have something that no one else knew about. McGraw had made me feel weak and dependent. The key gave me back some of my strength.

The McGraws had gone out to dinner by the time I reached Graham Court. Ralph let me in with his passkey. When I heard the apartment door later that evening, I snapped off my light so they would think I was asleep. I ignored a gentle tap on my door. It swung open, and I could smell Mrs. McGraw's soapy perfume. She eased the door closed and walked away.

Come morning, I thought I'd try to sneak out before the McGraws got up. I dressed without a sound and crept down the hallway, carrying my shoes in my hand. As I passed the kitchen, John McGraw called, "Come in here, please, Hank."

I thought of running, but I didn't want McGraw thinking I was afraid of him. So I stuck my head through the doorway. "Aren't you going to say good morning?" he asked. I looked at the floor. "Don't tell me you're a sore loser. Did Babe Ruth teach you that, too—to sulk when you're beaten?"

"Nobody pitches batting practice like that. You wanted to make a fool of me."

McGraw's face softened. "No, Hank. Babe Ruth is

making a fool of you. I just showed you what will happen if you try to hit that way. Wouldn't you rather learn it in private, between you and me, than in front of a crowd?"

Now he was trying to make it sound like he'd done me a favor. I clammed up again. McGraw sighed. "Anyway, I know it's my fault. I left you on your own too much. Half of America thinks Ruth is the greatest. How could I expect you not to?"

I met his gaze. "Babe wants to win, same as you. He's got different ways to do it, that's all."

"Wrong ways," McGraw insisted. "You'll see that when you're older. For now, I want you to go back to school. Finish out the year, and you and I will get a fresh start in June."

"I hate Anson Academy."

"Then go right here in the city. There's a school two blocks from here. We can sign you up this morning."

"Who's going to take care of Bill Pennant?"

"You can still do your job. Feed him before school in the morning, and check on him afterwards. You'll get to see a few innings of each game. You just won't have all that extra time to hang around and come under bad influences."

"School prepares a man for work. My work is baseball. The things I need to know I learn in the ballpark."

"Hank, I'm not asking. I'm sending you to school for your own good."

"I won't go."

McGraw rubbed a hand over his eyes. "Don't defy me, Hank. You can't stay under my roof and not do as I say."

"Then I won't stay." I turned and walked toward the

front door, moving slow so McGraw had plenty of time to call me back. He didn't.

Midmorning, having fed Billy, I hopped on the American Flyer one last time and rode it to Graham Court. Wheeling it into the lobby, I asked Jimmy the doorman if anyone was home.

"Nope. Himself is off to Brooklyn for the game, and the missus is out shopping."

I borrowed his key and went up to my room. It didn't take long to gather up the few clothes I hadn't left at Anson Academy. Most everything else I owned was either at the boarding school or in my locker at the Polo Grounds.

Down in the lobby, I left the Flyer in the storage closet, giving one last shine to those fancy rims. "Aren't you riding your cycle, Hank?" Jimmy asked, staring at the bundle of clothes under my arms.

"I'm returning it. John McGraw and I are on the outs."

"Are you leaving?"

"I'm not going far. I'll still work at the Polo Grounds, just for the Yankees now."

"But where will you stay?"

"With a friend."

"If you're stuck for a day or two, I can talk to my wife about letting you sleep on the couch."

"Thanks, I'll be fine." I pulled my cap over my eyes so he wouldn't see how watery they were getting and walked out.

At the Polo Grounds, I took the Giants gear out of my

locker and crammed my clothes into the space. I folded my uniform and sweater and set them on John McGraw's desk. I was leaving the office when I remembered my cap. I pulled it off and sailed it across the room. It landed on top of the pile.

By the time I was dressed as a Yankee, players were straggling in. When Babe hobbled in on crutches, most of his teammates gathered around to wish him well. Carl Mays shook his head and went onto the field to jog.

"How's it feel, Babe?" I asked once the others had gone out to warm up.

"Sore, but getting better. I can probably play in a day or two—if the Colonel will let me."

"So you are suspended?"

"I will be. Miller Huggins came to the hospital. Once he saw I was all right, he laid into me. Says Colonel Ruppert is backing him up. If I don't show respect, I don't play."

"How long will the suspension last?"

Babe sighed. "It's indefinite. Huggins says he'll lift it when he thinks I've learned my lesson."

That day the team won without Babe, nipping the Washington Senators by a score of 3–2. I squirmed through the game, hoping the Yankees would do well, but not so well that they decided they didn't need Ruth.

After the game, I fed Billy, then chowed down myself. The concessions sold hot dogs at a discount to folks who worked in the ballpark. I helped O'Hara and his crew sweep the stands. When everyone else started to file out, I fell behind, then sat on the floor in the middle of a row of seats near the left field line. I pulled the Spalding Guide from my pocket and read until I was sure even O'Hara had gone home.

Then I went onto the field and used my key to enter the scoreboard. I was used to overnighting in a ballpark after spring training in San Antonio. There were bathrooms, showers, everything a guy might need. I pulled a zero out of the first inning slot and breathed in the delicious spring air. It was dusky dark, and the outfield grass was a rich, deep green that darkened moment by moment to black.

I settled in the old wooden chair the scoreboard operator used, my feet resting on a shelf, and pulled my Yankees cap over my eyes. Sometime during the night, I must have lowered myself to the floor, because that's where I awoke, cold and stiff, to the sound of rain driving against the scoreboard.

Rain and Runyon

I changed into my civvies, keeping on my Yankees cap, and went down the street for breakfast. By the time I got to the diner, I was soaked. I planned to drink enough coffee to steam dry my clothes from the inside out.

I was hunkered in a booth, reading Runyon's column in the *American*, when a voice said, "Boy, that Runyon can write, can't he?"

I looked up. "Damon, you're here early."

"Raining too hard to sleep. Thought I'd have some breakfast, then interview a player or two before the game is called off and everyone scatters. I've still got a space to fill in the paper, even when nothing happens." He stopped at the counter long enough to order breakfast and get a mug of coffee, then slid in opposite me. "What's your excuse? I thought a fancy place like Graham Court would have soundproofing to keep the rain from waking McGraw."

"I'm not living there anymore."

Runyon's look made me sorry I'd owned up. "Where are you staying, Hank?"

"With a friend."

"Don't tell me it's Babe Ruth. I hear you two have been hanging around together."

"No, just a friend." Runyon had his reporter's eyes on me, and I kept my cap low so he couldn't read my expression.

"Something is bothering you, Hank. Is Bill Pennant all right?"

"He's fine, cranky as ever." I hesitated then figured Damon might have answers for some of the questions that were plaguing me. "Can we talk without it getting in the papers?"

Runyon held his open palms in front of him. "I'm off duty until I reach the ballpark."

"Why does John McGraw hate Babe Ruth?"

Runyon walked over to the rack of newspapers at the diner's door, while I fetched our plates of eggs from the counter. He held up each of the New York dailies so that the back page—the sports page—faced me. "Whose name is in the headlines?" he asked.

Every paper had a story on Babe Ruth, mostly speculation on how long his suspension would last, and could the Yankees live without him. I said, "Babe Ruth."

"For the past twenty years, McGraw's name would

have been in those headlines. What did he say to the umpire? Who did he challenge to a fight? How did he outsmart the opposition? Which of his players earned a tongue-lashing?" Runyon sat back down. "McGraw's not the biggest thing in New York anymore, and he doesn't like it."

"He's jealous?"

"That's part of it," Runyon admitted. "But it's more like he feels betrayed. How could people turn on him after all these years and embrace a player so much his opposite?"

"I betrayed him, too. He comes back from Boston and sees a picture in the paper of me wearing a Yankee uniform." I told Damon what had happened when McGraw pitched batting practice (although I might have left out the part where I fell flat on my back) and about our argument at the apartment.

"I've got to agree with McGraw on one thing, Hank," Damon said when I finished. "You should be in school."

That got my dander up, but before I could argue, the door opened, and two men in suits ducked inside and added to the puddle in the doorway. They spotted Runyon and came over to our booth. I sopped up the last of my egg yolk with a piece of toast and slid out. "See you at the ballpark," I said to Runyon.

"If Ruth gets there before I do, tell him I want to talk to him," Runyon said.

The rain cooled my temper. Runyon had made sense until he came out with that school crack. When I thought about all McGraw had done for me, I realized how he could feel betrayed. I wasn't about to let him boss me around, but I did wish there was something I could do to show him that I was grateful.

The storm had Bill Pennant restless. He paced in his cage, hair bristling, tail straight in the air. The full dish of sardines was smacked from my hand the second I pushed it through the feeding door. I decided to rake the sawdust in the bottom of his cage when he was in a better mood.

The players arrived, but no one got into uniform. They sat playing cards and checkers, confident that the game would be called. Babe joined the card game, propping his sore leg on an empty bench that I set alongside him.

After an hour or so, Huggins poked his head in and announced that the rainout was official. "We'll play two tomorrow, men, first pitch at noon. Be here by ten o'clock sharp."

The players filed out, half debating what movie to see on their afternoon off, and half complaining about the long day the doubleheader would bring. When Huggins passed through, he hesitated, as if waiting for Ruth to say something. I poked the Babe in the ribs, but he ignored me and let the manager leave without a word of apology.

Babe dug a sack of peanuts out of his coat pocket and set it on the bench between us, motioning me to dig in. The locker room was quiet except for the snap of the shells and the occasional sound from Ruth's overworked digestive system.

We tossed the shells on the floor. As we neared the bottom of the sack, some of the meaty sweetness faded as I thought what a pain it would be to clean up the mess.

Just as Babe spat out a dark one, Runyon's voice said, "Babe, I've heard a lot of stories about you, but no one ever told me you worked for peanuts."

"It's my day off. Why would I want to talk to you?" Ruth asked.

"If you don't, there will be a big hole in the sports page tomorrow." Runyon noticed Babe's face. "You haven't looked this glum since Prohibition started. What's the matter?"

"You know what's eating me. A man gets suspended for trying to help his team and then has to read your wisecracks."

"Come on, Babe. There's more going on here than bad base running. What did I miss?"

"Am I talking to a friend or a reporter?"

"Level with me, Babe, and I'll keep it out of the paper. I hate being in the dark."

So Babe told Runyon about the Locomobile. I even tipped my hat to show the egg on my noggin, although it wasn't nearly as impressive as it had been. "In two days, Ruppert heard complaints from one squirt who sells cars, and another who's supposed to be my boss. He treated me pretty square at contract time, and so far, he hasn't gotten anything for his money. I don't blame him for sitting me down."

"Does he know how you feel?" Runyon asked.

"Nah, but I'd like to make it up to him. Anything so he'll let me back in the lineup when this knee heals."

Runyon tipped his hat back and thought. "You know what you should do, Babe? Give him a present."

"A present? The guy owns a baseball team and a brewery. What more could he want?"

"That's just it," Runyon said, getting excited by his own idea. "Everybody takes from a rich man. Nobody ever thinks to give him something, make him feel appreciated."

"What could I give him? I don't even know what he likes."

Runyon rubbed his chin. "He likes sailing and he likes animals. He owns an estate along the Hudson River in Garrison where he raises horses, dogs, even monkeys."

"Monkeys? Are you kidding me?" Babe laughed.

An idea hit me so hard it nearly knocked off my Yankee cap. "If he likes wild animals, I've got the perfect gift." Runyon and Ruth stared at me. "McGraw's given up on Bill Pennant. He told me he wants to find a home for him before the Giants come back from their road trip."

"Do you want to try it, Babe?" Runyon asked. "If the Colonel likes your present, he'll go easy on you. If he doesn't like it, Bill Pennant may do away with him. Either way you're off the hook."

"How far is Garrison?" Babe asked.

"More than an hour," Runyon answered. "But I've got my Packard outside, and we've got the whole day."

"It's raining so hard that if we fall off the ferry, we won't even know it," Babe grumbled. But he heaved himself to his feet.

The Gift

T he way Billy behaved nowadays, I knew he would hide in the travel crate when he heard us coming. I figured we could empty the ball bats out of a canvas sack and load Billy's doorless travel crate into it. That way we could get him into the car without being mauled. The hard part was convincing Damon Runyon to hold the sack.

"Babe can't do it with one good leg," I argued, "and I don't think you want to be the person who reaches into the cage for him."

Runyon muttered, "It's a lot more fun writing about other people's stupidity than living with your own." But he stood at the front of Billy's cage with the sack spread wide. As quietly as possible, I began unhooking the front panel. Once the cage was open, Babe and I would each grab one side of Billy's travel crate and slide it into the sack. All Runyon had to do was cinch the drawstrings, and we'd be ready to go.

I loosened the last hook from its eye and nodded to Babe. We lifted the front of the cage free and bent to set it on the floor, the crutch Babe held under one arm slowing us down some. With a snarl of fury, Bill Pennant launched himself from the travel crate, claws extended and aimed for Runyon's nose. Damon jerked his arms upward in panic, and by some miracle, Billy dove into the sack. It flew from Runyon's grip, but I pounced on it before Billy could escape. His claws raked the inside of the thick canvas as Damon knotted the drawstrings, closing the top.

The three of us lay on the floor, sweat running down our faces, while Billy used up the rest of his energy. "And you think the Colonel is going to want this critter?" Babe asked.

Runyon shrugged. "He hired you, didn't he? He must like challenges."

When the commotion in the sack died, I grabbed the drawstrings and hoisted the bag over my shoulder. The darkness must have calmed him, because Bill Pennant made no fuss as I carried him out to Runyon's car.

The ferry crossing and drive to Garrison gave Runyon plenty of time to tell us about the Yankees' owner, Jacob Ruppert. The conversation helped, because it was raining too hard to enjoy the scenery. To my relief, Runyon drove like he planned on getting home alive. After being Babe Ruth's passenger, I had started the trip with my feet braced against the back of the front seat. But I soon relaxed.

"Jacob Ruppert likes to be called Colonel, but he's not a real soldier," Runyon began. "He's in the National Guard and marches reserves up and down the street for a few weeks each year. Brewmaster would be a better title for him."

"When I signed my contract, he was bragging about the great beer his family makes," Babe said.

"Made, you mean," Runyon said. "With Prohibition the brewery is shut down. But he has so many millions socked away that I don't think he notices."

Even with the rain, we cracked our windows. Bill Pennant still wasn't a good traveler. I had kept the drawstrings loose so Billy could breathe, and gagging sounds and bad odors seeped from the canvas sack. I figured it was a good time to turn the talk to baseball. "Who do you think will win the pennant?" I asked Runyon.

"Tough to say. The White Sox are loaded. If they play all out this year, they'll probably take it again."

"We can beat those bums," Babe said.

Runyon ignored him. "Then there's Cleveland. Tris Speaker's the best center fielder in the game, and a fine manager to boot. No one plays shortstop like Ray Chapman. If their pitching holds up, they'll be hard to beat."

"Cleveland?" Babe hooted. "I can beat those Indians on one leg."

The rain had let up enough to look out the window. I caught a brief glimpse of the Hudson River. Then it was screened by a fancy, black iron fence running along the side of the road.

"That's Ruppert's fence," Runyon said. "He owns all this land." It seemed we drove a mile or more, fence posts spinning past until my eyes blurred. Then Runyon slowed and pulled up to a massive iron gate enclosed by a pair of stone pillars.

"Looks like nobody's home," Babe said. "Kid, if you brought us all the way up here for nothing, I'm going to stuff you in the sack with the wildcat."

"He's home," Runyon said. "You didn't think we were going to stroll up to the front door, did you? Hank, there's a button on the right-hand pillar. Push it, and when they ask who you are, give Babe's name."

"Tell them I'm hungry, too," Babe added.

I pulled my cap down, turned my collar up, and climbed out of the car. A strong wind blew rain into my face. I found the button easy enough. Nothing happened when I pushed it, so I held it down. Soaked to the skin, I let go and turned to get back in the car. Then I heard a voice. "Keep your finger off the button or you will not be able to hear me. Depress the button to speak. Who is causing this disturbance?"

"Babe Ruth," I answered, "to see Colonel Ruppert."

"Young man, I am calling the police. I met the great Babe Ruth when he signed a contract with the Yankees. Your adolescent squawk bears no resemblance to the rich timbre of his voice."

At the mention of police, I nearly bolted. I knew from my wandering years that some cops hit first and asked

questions later, especially if rich people complained about
you. Then I remembered that I was with Damon Runyon
and Babe Ruth. There wasn't a cop in New York who
didn't know their names. I pushed the button again. "My
name is Hank Cobb. I'm speaking for Babe Ruth. Does he
have to stand in the rain so you can hear him?"

After a pause, the voice said, "Wait there."

I got back in the car. "How's the water?" Babe asked.

I ignored him and wrung out my cap on the floor
mats. "Whoever was at the other end of that thing said
for us to wait," I reported.

A few minutes later, a car came down the driveway. A
man in a chauffeur's uniform got out, unlocked the gates,
and swung them open. Runyon steered the Packard
through, tipping his porkpie hat as we passed.

He drove up a long, curved road under giant trees. We
rounded a bend and saw the front of a house the size of
the Natural History Museum. The driveway wound past a
lawn with a marble fountain. We stopped under a roofed
porch and were met by a man in a suit who peered inside
the car. He recognized the Babe and scrambled to open
his door. Runyon and I let ourselves out. I trailed the
group up a flight of painted wooden steps to the entrance.

"The Colonel will receive you in his study," the character who had led us in explained. "Be careful of Pilsner."

That last remark concerned a massive, brown-and-
white St. Bernard that lay in the middle of the floor. I
knew it wasn't dead from the snoring. We stepped over
Pilsner and trooped down a dark hallway lined with
paintings of odd-looking people. I expect they were

related to each other since they all had the same sour expression on their faces.

Why would folks who looked like that bunch allow their portraits to be painted? Nowadays, a careless soul might get caught unawares by a photographer, like I had at the Polo Grounds. But if somebody started painting your picture, and you didn't want it, you could crawl away if you had to.

We got past the rogues' gallery and were waved into the Colonel's study. It was the finest room I had ever seen. Two walls were covered by polished wooden bookcases that shot all the way to the ceiling, broken only by the doorway we had passed through. There were wheeled ladders attached to them that slid back and forth so that any book you wanted was within your grasp.

The back wall, which faced the Hudson River, was glass. All I could see at the moment were branches waving in the wind. But I'll bet the view was spectacular on a clear day.

Giant stones formed the entire fourth wall, which sported a fireplace large enough to roast a cow. The fire was a perfect size, taking the chill off the room without making you want to strip to your skivvies. A long, leather couch faced the flames, and we flopped down on its warm cushions. The place smelled like a well-oiled baseball mitt.

The tables were cluttered with framed photographs of Colonel Ruppert doing rich man things like inspecting his troops, pouring a glass of the family suds, and riding a horse. There was even one where he was sailing a boat on the ocean. I couldn't believe a person could make so much money from selling beer. But then I thought of how the old man could put it away. If a fellow had a few hundred customers like him, he'd be set for life.

Runyon popped up from the couch and wandered the room, studying its treasures. Babe was content to stare into the fire and massage his sore knee. Our ears perked up at what sounded like a pack of coyotes coming down the hall. The door opened, and there was the Colonel, surrounded by a half-dozen small, smooth-haired dogs with ugly faces.

The dogs raced around the room inspecting each of us in turn. One let out a yelp when he smelled my feet, and I hoped I hadn't stepped in anything on the way in. Judging by the size of that St. Bernard snoozing by the front door, a person would be smart to watch his step around here. A speckled dog gnawed the tip of one of Babe's crutches, until he prodded it with his toe.

When the dogs had calmed and lay on the warm stone in front of the fire, I eyeballed the owner of the Yankees. He wore itchy-looking trousers and a thick, woolen shirt. His gray hair and mustache were freshly trimmed. The Colonel said to Babe Ruth, "George, this is a surprise."

Babe struggled to his feet and stuck out his hand. "Good to see you, Colonel. I came to apologize for . . ." He seemed unsure what to say and waved a crutch by way of explanation.

"Injuries are part of the game, George. It's how you were hurt that concerns me."

"I know." Babe sighed. "I thought I'd catch those A's by surprise, shake things up a bit."

"Surprises should be sprung by Miller Huggins. He plans strategy. You, George, are to do what he says, and nothing more."

"I will, Colonel. I've learned my lesson." Ruppert looked unconvinced.

Damon Runyon walked over and introduced himself. "Does this mean I'll be reading about my home in the newspaper? I don't know that I like that," Ruppert said.

"No, Colonel," Runyon assured him. "I'll respect your privacy. All I want to print is that Babe Ruth will be back in the lineup as soon as he's healthy enough to play. That will be my scoop."

Babe looked in my direction, and I held my hands up like a set of claws. "Oh yeah, I brought you a gift," Babe said.

Colonel Ruppert sighed. "The only gift I want is your cooperation, George. I thought I had purchased that when you signed your contract."

"Hank, run out to the car and get it," Runyon said in the awkward silence that followed. I found my way to the door, unable to resist doing a dance step in front of Pilsner. He didn't even blink. Luckily, the car was where we had left it. I guess the help wanted it handy in case Ruppert gave us the heave-ho. I opened the rear door and nearly gagged. After his bout of motion sickness, Billy wasn't the most fragrant present.

I threw the sack over my shoulder, slammed the car door, and went inside. Just as I was stepping over Pilsner, his nose twitched. He let loose a howl and lurched to his feet, sending me crashing to the floor. Bill Pennant yowled in shock as the canvas sack flew from my hands and slid down the slippery hallway.

Pilsner scrambled over me, our legs entangling as he tried to reach the sack. Somehow, I got to my feet just as the six smaller dogs raced down the hall, eager to get in on the excitement. I grabbed the sack and heaved it onto my back, Bill Pennant hissing and snarling. I ran through the pack toward the Colonel's study while the dogs skidded in the wrong direction. I made it as far as the doorway, where Ruppert, Runyon, and Ruth stood frozen. Then I was bowled over from behind by Pilsner. The sack shot across the room, the top popped open, and out came Bill Pennant, tail bristling and eyes twice their usual size.

Billy leaped onto a table, leaving deep claw marks in its gleaming surface. Framed photographs crashed to the floor as he sprang from one piece of furniture to another, the maddened dogs in hot pursuit. He scaled a bookcase, showering us with books and knickknacks. At last, he curled into a ball on the top shelf, launching a model sailboat that knocked a globe of the world from its stand. The small dogs joined Pilsner in leaping and howling at the base of the bookcase. More photos and doodads crashed to the floor. We added to the confusion by banging into each other and the furnishings, trying to grab the dogs.

"Suds, Amber, Foamy, Stein, Mug, Hops, Pilsner! Get down!" Colonel Ruppert barked. Those dogs probably had fancy papers, but the presence of Bill Pennant had them behaving like the lowliest mutts. Only when the small dogs were picked up and toted out of the room by the four of us, and two servants had dragged Pilsner into the hallway, did things calm down.

We sank to the couch, wiping sweat from our foreheads. Bill Pennant continued hissing from the top shelf, his fur puffed out as if he had been given an electric shock. No one said anything for a while. Then Colonel Ruppert put his arm on Babe's shoulder. "Is he really mine to keep, George?" he asked.

Pennantless 18

A bell tinkled in the distance, interrupting Ruppert's description of the huge outdoor cage he was going to have built for Bill Pennant. He cocked an ear and said, "Gentlemen, please accompany me to the dining room." Babe was quite lively on his crutches, beating Runyon and me to the door. Two glum-faced servants were left behind, holding Billy's sack in case he left his perch.

I wasn't expecting much as the Colonel hadn't known we were coming. But the dining room table groaned from an assortment of roasted meats, vegetables, and a lot of dishes I didn't know the names of. Call me crazy, but I could have sworn there were fish eggs in one bowl. Dinner plates sparkled under a crystal chandelier until we buried them in so much food that it killed the glow.

I ate till I was bursting, sticking to things I recognized.

When I came up for air, I saw that Runyon and the Colonel had reached their limit and were discussing the Yankees' chances. Babe was doing horrible things to a drumstick. At last, even he pushed his chair back from the table. "That eats good, Colonel," he said. Runyon and I added our thanks.

When we stood to leave, Ruppert said, "Stay overnight, gentlemen. I'll take you on a tour of the stables in the morning."

Runyon explained that he and the Babe had obligations in the city. I was about to say that I had to get back and feed Bill Pennant when I remembered that responsibility wasn't mine anymore.

"Does this mean you and me are square?" Babe asked Ruppert.

"George, the moment your leg has healed, I want you in the lineup. I'll tell Huggins tomorrow."

Several members of the Colonel's staff passed by armed with brooms, mops, and dustpans to clean up the mess that Bill Pennant and the dogs had made. All of them, including the man who showed us to the door, gave us dirty looks. I guess they were anticipating the extra work that Billy would cause. Those looks bounced right off me. I felt free for the first time in a month.

"Let me sit in the back this time, Kid," Babe said. By the time we had eased down the driveway and were turning onto Route 9, he was snoring. The rain picked up, so Runyon didn't have much time for small talk. While he peered between the windshield wipers, I thought over the day's events. The closer we got to New York City, the less sure I was that John McGraw would be happy with what I had done.

Runyon did a double take when I asked to be dropped at Graham Court, but he kept his thoughts to himself. Ralph spotted me getting out at the curb and swung the door open. "Are you back, Hank?" he asked.

"Just visiting," I answered.

"If you hurry, you can catch them at the dinner table."

I couldn't even think about food after all I had eaten, but I was glad. Even my old man was in a good mood after a feed. I couldn't hope for a better time to talk to McGraw.

It felt strange, but I knocked on the door. A minute later, John McGraw pulled it open. We stared at each other until he said, "Well, Hank, you're a little wet, but otherwise no worse for the wear. Have you come home?"

"No, sir. I just wanted to tell you that I found a new owner for Bill Pennant."

"Are you joking? Who would take him?"

"I . . . gave him to Colonel Ruppert."

McGraw's eyebrows lifted in surprise. I got on the balls of my feet, in case I needed to duck and run. Then his face lit with the biggest smile I had seen on it since the day he introduced me to Bill Pennant. "Hank, you're a genius. If Billy doesn't put the jinx on those Yankees, I don't know what will."

He threw an arm over my shoulder and half dragged me to the dining room. I started to explain how full I was, but my eye was caught by a strawberry-rhubarb pie, puffs of steam wafting from the crust. It reminded me that I hadn't really had dessert.

Mrs. McGraw fussed over me and made sure to add a dollop of heavy cream to my slice of pie. McGraw was beaming, chuckling to himself between sips of coffee. I took advantage of the moment. "I'm hoping you'll let me keep my job at the Polo Grounds. I can run down foul balls for both teams and help Smoky whenever the Giants are in town."

"Are you determined not to go back to school?" McGraw asked.

"Yes, sir. The ballpark is my classroom." I didn't mention that it was my dormitory also.

"I quit school myself, Hank," McGraw admitted, "and got away with it. I was lucky. For every baseballer who makes it big like I did, there are hundreds who fall on their faces. I don't approve, so you can't live here. But I won't force you to do something you don't want."

"That's all I ask." I shoved my chair back and turned to Mrs. McGraw. "Thanks for the pie. It was great."

"Won't you tell us where you're living, Hank? Is it clean and safe?"

"You'd spend time there yourself, ma'am," I assured her.

John McGraw walked me to the door. "Remember what I taught you, Hank. This power hitting is a flash in the pan. Baseball is a game of brains, not brawn."

It was sad to see a man stuck in the past. I didn't want to argue, so I said, "Good luck on the road trip."

Babe's Barrage

abe Ruth returned to the Yankee lineup on May 1 for a game against the Red Sox. That sunny Saturday afternoon, the bugs packing the Polo Grounds greeted him like a returning hero. Herb Pennock, Boston's finest, was on the mound, but Babe was not to be denied. He hit a towering fly ball into the second deck of stands in right field. At long last he had that first home run of the season. His teammates joined the fun, and the Yankees won 6–0.

Have you ever struggled to get the ketchup out of a new bottle? It seems that you'll never get a drop, then suddenly, your eggs are buried. That's the way home runs were for Ruth. Once he popped that first one, the floodgates opened. Babe hit a dozen home runs in June, more than enough to lead the league for the whole season in most previous years. And, the hotter Babe got, the more games the Yankees won. Everyone from Ping Bodie to Wally Pipp was ripping the ball.

The more I watched Babe thrill the bugs, the more I wanted to be a home run hitter myself. Whenever I could, I'd get one of O'Hara's sons or nephews to pitch to me. I copied Babe's uppercut swing. I wasn't big enough to reach the fences yet, but I was hitting some long fly balls.

On July 17, the Yankees faced the White Sox. Both teams sent out ace pitchers who were having sensational seasons. Carl Mays gave up five runs. Facing the great Eddie Cicotte, you would think that guaranteed a loss. Think again. The Yankees won the game 20–5. And the Babe? He hit two home runs, his thirtieth and thirty-first of the year, breaking the all-time record he had set just last season.

When I got done rubbing my eyes and pinching myself to make sure I wasn't dreaming, I thought back to the day I met Babe Ruth. He had said he would have hit fifty home runs if he had played in the Polo Grounds in 1919, and I had laughed. Now it was hard to imagine Babe not having that many by the end of the season.

The Giants couldn't get a streak going. On July 23, while the Yankees were moving into first place, the Giants were mired in fourth with forty-one wins and forty-three losses. The bugs were still supporting McGraw's team. The Giants led the National League in attendance. But the Yankees were selling tickets in unheard-of numbers. Three times they broke the Polo

Grounds' single-game attendance record, which now stood at close to thirty-nine thousand. The Giants had never played before that many people, not even in the World Series. New Yorkers couldn't get enough of Babe Ruth.

The better the Yankees played, the madder John McGraw got. I knew not to mention Babe Ruth's name in his presence. But some of the reporters did it just to agitate him. He was quoted in one paper as saying, "Sluggers play a dull, brainless game that will soon bore the bugs. Without strategy, baseball is nothing." The more the Yankees won, the more McGraw's attitude seemed like sour grapes.

I had asked to be treated as an employee, and that's just what John McGraw did. He ordered me around, seldom calling me by name. Sometimes I'd catch him staring at me, and it would cross my mind that he might miss our old relationship as much as I did. Then I'd think how tough he was and know that couldn't be true.

Summer was passing in a blur of cheering fans, sizzling hot dogs, and booming drives off Babe Ruth's bat. When the Giants were in town, Smoky and I played checkers and talked baseball. When they were on the road, I had the Babe and Damon Runyon for company. And at night, I had that whole, beautiful ballpark to myself. If there was enough breeze to keep the insects from landing, I'd lie on the outfield grass and stare up at the sky until I fell asleep. I had all the fun of camping out, with the luxury of a shower, a bathroom, and a locker full of clothes. Anytime I was hungry, I had enough money in my pocket to fill my belly with whatever food the neighborhood joints offered. Generally, I stuck to bacon and eggs for breakfast, hot dogs for lunch and dinner, and fresh fruit from the street peddlers for snacks.

Every day I felt bigger and stronger. It seemed like I had finally gotten life figured out. I'd keep soaking up baseball and growing for another year or two. Then it would be my turn to be the hot young slugger.

The Pro Must Go On

ithout warning, it began to look as if John McGraw had been right about things all along. The Giants were making a move. Second baseman Larry Doyle, who had been on the team longer than anyone else, was playing like a kid. George Burns, Pep Youngs, and the other outfielders were catching anything that stayed in the ballpark. The pitchers were basking in the August heat, their arms limber.

John McGraw was everywhere. He knew just when to rattle the other team with a stolen base. If he signaled for a hit-and-run, the batter came through with a ground ball to the right spot. McGraw called every pitch the Giants hurlers threw, and he was a master at keeping hitters off balance. In one game, he had the great Rogers Hornsby flailing away almost as wildly as I had in the batting practice that had built a wall between McGraw and me.

On Monday, August 16, I sat reading the sports page in a greasy spoon a block from the ballpark. The Giants were on their way to Philadelphia, and I was going to spend the day watching the Yankees battle the Cleveland Indians. I stared at the standings until my eyes watered, but they didn't change. In the National League, the Giants were in third place, two and a half games out of first. In the American League, the Yankees were in third place, two and a half games out of first. How had McGraw done it?

Damon Runyon was the first to imagine in print what it would be like if the Yankees and the Giants both won the pennant and faced each other in the World Series. He wrote that the World Series had been going on since 1903. In 1906, two teams from the same city had played—the White Sox and the Cubs. But if the Yankees and the Giants met, the championship would be between teams who shared not only a city, but a ballpark. *The Polo Grounds has been the site of some thrilling baseball this season, but it is hard to conjure up the electricity that would flow through the stadium if landlord and tenant met in the World Series.*

The idea had me squirming. But first the Giants would have to catch the world champion Cincinnati Reds and the Brooklyn Robins, and the Yankees would have to overtake the White Sox and the Indians. I swallowed my eggs so fast, I don't think I broke the yolks. I couldn't wait to get to the ballpark.

I had another reason for getting to the Polo Grounds

early. Carl Mays was pitching. If Mays was as surly as a hungry Bill Pennant on a normal day, he was at his worst when it was his turn to pitch. I planned to be in uniform with the bats and equipment laid out before he showed up. Then I would concentrate on staying out of his path. When he was stretching in the locker room, I'd be on the diamond chasing foul balls and wild throws. When he came out to the sidelines to warm up, I'd clean the locker room or sit in the dugout.

I broke into a sweat as soon as I reached the street. The air was so thick that I felt like I was swimming. It was the kind of day when your woolen uniform got heavier with each inning that passed. Rain might have cooled things down, but the last thing I wanted was for the game to be called off, so I couldn't wish for a shower.

My plan for avoiding Carl Mays worked perfectly. I watched from the dugout as he warmed up. The sticky weather seemed to agree with him, his pitches crashing into Muddy Ruel's mitt with a loud slap. Even after a whole season, I couldn't watch Mays work without a tingle of fear crawling through my stomach. I was sure that if I ever hit against him, I'd flinch on every pitch.

When Mays signaled that his arm was loose, I left the dugout. By the time he was seated on the bench, I was squatting along the left field foul line, a great angle to watch the Indians take batting practice.

There were two players I especially wanted to see. The Indians' manager, Tris Speaker, was their best hitter. He didn't knock them over the fence like the Babe, but he hit a ton of doubles and triples. Despite the fact that he had been playing for over ten years, he was still the fastest runner on the team. The Grey Eagle, as Runyon called him, could go and get a fly ball with the best of them.

Ray Chapman was Cleveland's other star. Chappie was the best shortstop in the majors, sure-handed and strong-armed. At bat, he was the kind of player John McGraw loved. He hit the ball to all fields, seldom struck out, and was a skilled bunter.

Rumor had it that Chapman was going to retire after the season, even though he was only twenty-nine years old. Ray had recently gotten married. His girl's father was a business tycoon, and Chappie was giving up the diamond to work in an office. I don't know how he could stand the thought of it.

I was waiting for the Indians to take the field when Chapman came to the top step of the dugout. He faced his seated teammates and, of all things, started to sing. "In the shade of the old apple tree . . ."

First one, then another teammate joined in, until the squad was in full voice. By the time they reached the end of the song, hundreds of bugs were warbling along with them. Finishing with a flourish, Chappie swept his cap from his head, took a bow, and led his laughing teammates onto the field. Talk about taking off the pressure in a pennant race. No wonder his teammates loved him. I couldn't help but imagine what it would be like to hang around the Cleveland dugout with no Carl Mays to poison things.

In batting practice, Speaker ripped the ball to all fields. I snagged one that he blistered down the line. My hand stung as if I had caught it barehanded. I noticed that every Indian ran full tilt to first base when his turn at bat was done. Speaker had them hustling.

When the Indians disappeared into their dugout, I took off my glove and massaged my palm. Speaker's ball had raised a welt. Tommy Connolly, an umpire who took no lip from anyone, dusted off home plate. A bat boy offered him a megaphone. Connolly shook his head as if to ask, "What for?" and bellowed, "Play ball!" loud enough to be heard in Brooklyn. It started to drizzle, but I don't know if Connolly's booming shout had caused that or not.

The Yankees streamed out of their dugout, Babe Ruth winking as he trotted past me to his position in left field. Carl Mays trudged to the mound, a sour expression on his puss. The lead-off batter smacked a single, Chappie bunted him to second, and Speaker came to the plate. Before I had time to get nervous, Mays got Tris and the following batter on soft fly balls to center field.

Mays looked sharp, but so did Cleveland starter Stanley Coveleski. Unlike most spitball pitchers, Coveleski had great control. Huggins claimed that he had once made it to the seventh inning without throwing a pitch out of the strike zone. I could almost believe that stretcher watching the way he handled the Yankees.

Steve O'Neill hit a homer in the third to give the Indians the lead. The ball hooked just inside the left field foul pole despite Babe waving his arms and me leaning to make it go foul. In the fourth inning, the infielders kicked the ball around, letting two more runs score. Mays looked mad enough to bite his glove in half.

The drizzle stopped for the fifth inning. The Yankees trailed 3–0, and Mays had to face the Indians' best hitters. Ray Chapman would lead off. Chappie had bunted in both his previous at-bats, and the infielders were on their toes in case he bunted again.

Mays wound, arms circling his head. He dipped low and whipped his arm toward the ground, releasing the ball from that lowest point. The baseball sped homeward, rising and curving as it flew. There was a strange thunk, and the ball bounced to Mays. Carl fielded it and threw to Wally Pipp at first base.

Wally raised his arm to throw the baseball around the horn. Something happening at home plate caught his eye, and the ball dropped from his hand. I craned my neck to see what Pipp had seen. Ray Chapman was collapsing. The bugs let out a moan that swept the stadium as they realized the baseball hadn't struck Chapman's bat. It had hit him in the head.

Muddy Ruel, the Yankees' catcher, wrapped his arms around Chappie as he sank to his knees. The Cleveland dugout emptied, players racing to their fallen teammate. I tried to run in myself, thinking I had to do something to help. My feet moved, but I stayed in the same place. Babe Ruth had hold of my belt. "Stay here, Kid. We're close enough," he said.

Reluctantly, I sat on the ground, the Babe next to me. We didn't say a word as Umpire Connolly faced the stands and bellowed, "We need a doctor!" Two men pushed through the crowd, vaulted the railing, and ran to home plate. One made the Cleveland players move back while the other bent over Chapman. The Polo Grounds was so quiet that it hurt my ears. I felt tears welling, so I kept my face turned away from the Babe. I didn't want him thinking I was a sissy.

After what seemed a lifetime, Speaker and another player helped Chapman to his feet. With the doctors following, they started the long walk to the gate in center field where a car waited to take Chappie to the hospital. Blood caked the left side of his face. Twenty thousand bugs stood and cheered.

Near second base, Chapman's legs buckled, and he fell again. Speaker and the other player linked hands under Ray's knees and carried him the rest of the way, his arms draped over their shoulders. When they reached the gate, they lowered Chapman onto the front seat of the car and closed the door. The doctors piled into the back.

As the car pulled away, the players trudged back to the diamond. O'Hara closed the gate. Babe squeezed my shoulder and walked to his position in left field.

At last, I thought to look for Carl Mays. The pitcher stood, arms folded, in front of the mound. He walked toward first base and picked up the baseball that had struck Chapman. Mays flipped the ball to Umpire Connolly, who looked it over, then tossed it into the dugout. Connolly threw Mays a new baseball, yelled, "Play ball!" and crouched behind the catcher.

I couldn't believe it. The game was going to continue as if nothing had happened. Tris Speaker pointed into the dugout, and a player trotted to first base to pinch-run for Ray Chapman. Speaker stepped into the batter's box and took his stance.

I stared at the field, but I don't remember a thing that happened for the rest of the game. When Babe Ruth offered his hand and lifted me to my feet, I followed him into the dugout. Only then did I notice that the bugs were leaving. I looked at the scoreboard and saw that the Yankees had scored three times in the ninth inning, but lost by a run.

"Did you hit one?" I asked.

"A lousy single. Are you all right, Kid?"

Questions poured out of me. "How did you guys go right back to playing? How could Speaker jump into the batter's box like nothing was wrong?"

"It's our job, Kid. That's what it means to be a pro."

"How could Mays pitch knowing he had almost killed someone?"

Babe shrugged and headed for the showers. I sat on the bench in the corner of the dugout. The rain settled in for real now, falling in heavy sheets until I could no longer see the outfield fence. I wedged my back against the wall, brought my feet up onto the bench, and wrapped my arms around my knees. The drumming of the rain was deafening, yet it couldn't drown out the thoughts that raced through my brain.

Wedding Cake Wake

21

I don't know how long I sat there. The rain had eased up, and the locker room fallen quiet behind me. I heard someone jump the railing near third base and walk in my direction. When he reached the top step of the dugout, I recognized Runyon's hat. "Hank? What are you doing here?"

"Thinking things over." I stood and stretched.

"A ballplayer's life doesn't look so great today, does it?" Runyon asked.

I didn't want to touch that one. I asked, "Why aren't you at the hospital?"

Runyon sighed. "I want to talk to Carl Mays—get his side of the story. I've been waiting by the players' entrance, but he never came out."

"You think he's still here?"

"I do, and I want you to tell him I'd like to talk to him."

"Me? Mays can't stand me on a good day."

"Go on, Hank. You'll be doing him a favor."

Runyon sat on the bench, waiting for me to obey. I felt like telling Carl Mays what I thought of him. What kind of man bounces a baseball off someone's head and goes back to work as if nothing had happened?

The locker room was dark, so I doubted Mays was in there. I walked toward the back. Huggins's office, McGraw's office, and Smoky's training room were locked up tight. Then I heard it—a low moaning sound coming from the showers. I tiptoed over and stuck my head into the big, open room where six shower nozzles pointed at a half-rotted wooden floor.

Carl Mays sat in the darkest, dampest corner, his shoulders shaking with sobs. His empty eyes stared, but gave no sign of seeing me. I turned and crept toward the dugout, praying I wouldn't trip and make noise.

When I reached Runyon, I said, "He must have gotten past you. There's no one in there."

"Huh. I guess I'm slipping," Runyon said. "Do you want a ride home?"

"I'll take one to that coffee shop a couple of blocks from here."

Runyon dropped me off. I sat in a booth with the late editions of a couple of newspapers, but I couldn't concentrate. I wondered if Chapman would still be a good ballplayer. Maybe he'd be afraid to go up to bat. It scared me to think that one pitch might end a career.

What about Cleveland's chances for the pennant?

Their biggest weakness was their bench, and now one of those yannigans would have to play every day while Chappie was healing.

It took a long time for me to fall asleep that night, and it wasn't just because the scoreboard room was damp and chilly. Chapman's knees buckled a thousand times before sunup. When I opened my eyes in the morning, I couldn't think of anything else. I showered and dressed in the locker room, keeping my back to the corner where Carl Mays had crouched, and left the ballpark before O'Hara or any of the other workers arrived.

I stopped for coffee and a roll and read Runyon's game story in the *American*. He called it an "accidental beaning" every time he mentioned the incident and closed by describing Chapman's condition as "extremely critical." I didn't know much about doctoring, but I knew that wasn't good.

I decided to walk to the Ansonia Hotel on Broadway where Babe Ruth lived. All the visiting teams stayed there, so I figured that would be the place to get the latest news on Chappie. If someone tried to run me off, I could say that I was there to see the Babe.

Ruth was as bad with place names as he was with people's. He called the Ansonia "that wedding cake on Broadway." The building was sixteen or seventeen stories high, made from concrete and stone. If you passed by on the sidewalk, it was like walking at the base of a mountain. But if you saw it from a distance, it looked as light and fluffy as a fancy dessert. The concrete was tipped with lacy frills. Balconies with iron railings as thin as licorice whips trimmed the sides. Faces of gods or monsters grinned down from the roof. A tower shot up at each end of the building, giving the whole caboodle the look of a castle in a fairy tale.

I had never been inside the Ansonia, but I strode up the stone steps and spun through the revolving door as if I were a daily visitor. The doorman eyeballed me, but didn't say anything. It was spookily quiet in the cavernous lobby. The only sound was the gurgle of water from a fountain that sat in the middle of the room.

At first I thought no one was around. I checked a wall clock with metal rays sticking out in all directions that, I guess, was supposed to look like the sun. It was just shy of eight o'clock. As my eyes adjusted to the dim light, I saw about twenty men scattered around the lobby, staring at the walls.

Now that I was here, I wasn't sure what to do. I crossed the lobby to ask the desk clerk for Babe Ruth's room number. As I got closer, I realized that the silent men were the Cleveland baseballers. I didn't see Speaker, but it seemed that the rest of the roster was here. From the looks of them, they hadn't been to bed all night.

A hand rested on my shoulder. I spun around to face a rumpled Babe Ruth. "If you're looking for me, come back later. I need a couple of hours sleep before I go to the ballpark."

Babe's breath had that sour smell I remembered from my old man's drinking days. But if Babe had been out all night, it hadn't made him mean. "Don't tell me you haven't been home yet, either, Kid," he joked.

Ruth spotted the players perched around the lobby and arched an eyebrow in concern. He approached Steve O'Neill, the man who had homered for the first run in yesterday's game, something that seemed like it had happened a hundred years ago. "How's Chappie?" Babe asked.

O'Neill shook his head.

"Is he hurt bad?" Babe persisted.

The pain in O'Neill's eyes sent a queer chill streaking through my body. "He's gone, Babe. Died at four o'clock this morning."

O'Neill was fighting tears. Babe didn't bother. He let loose a mighty sob that triggered my waterworks. When I got close enough, Babe wrapped me in his arms and leaned on my shoulder, tears streaming down his cheeks. All I could think was how full of life Chappie had looked, leading his team in song, and laughing at the pressure of a pennant race.

I managed to steer Babe to a couch. Babe's sobs slowed. I rubbed my face raw with my cap, trying to hide my tears. Babe got up, went to each of the Cleveland players, and whispered some form of "I'm sorry."

When he had worked his way around the lobby, he headed for the elevator. As the doors closed, he called, "See you at the ballpark, Kid."

I was too numb to move, so I sat with the Indians, none of us saying anything, but all seeming to draw comfort from each other's presence. When Damon Runyon came through the revolving doors, a couple of the players got up and left. Two others, Jack Graney and Doc Johnston, charged across the lobby to meet him.

"Put it in the paper that Carl Mays should be banned from baseball," Graney said.

Doc Johnston topped him. "He should be strung up."

Runyon stayed calm. "Now, you boys know he didn't hit Ray on purpose."

"Maybe not," admitted Graney, "but he's come close to me too many times. That weird delivery of his keeps the ball hidden until it's too late to react."

"What's his side of the story?" Doc Johnston asked.

"He blames Connolly," Runyon answered.

"The umpire?" half a dozen voices said at once.

"Carl says the ball was damaged, and that's why he lost control of it. He says it's the umpire's job to keep a safe ball in play."

"That's nonsense," Graney spat. "Mays has been marking up baseballs for years. The balls he's doctored could fill a stadium. Now he's complaining because he wasn't caught?"

"Has anyone told Connolly what he said?" Doc Johnston wondered.

Runyon nodded. "Connolly says that the league president ordered the umpires to use fewer baseballs. He threw the ball out after the beaning because Mays asked for a new one, but he didn't see anything wrong with it." All this blaming was making my head ache.

"I'll tell you what else Connolly said," Runyon went on. "He was set to call the pitch a strike when it hit Chapman. Ray leaned over the plate and didn't duck out of the way. My guess is that he never saw the ball."

That image left everyone quiet. There had been

thousands and thousands of pitches thrown in the major leagues, and none had ever ended a batter's life before. Johnston and Graney slumped onto a couch and hung their heads. Runyon tapped me on the shoulder, and I followed him outside.

The cops knew Runyon and let him park pretty much where he wanted, so it was a short walk to the Packard. "Hop in, Hank. I'll give you a ride to the ballpark."

I stopped dead. "Do you mean they're going to play today? Those Indians are in a daze. A bunch of school kids could whip them."

"Calm down, Hank. The game's been called off, but the bugs won't know it until the next edition of the paper comes out. I want to interview some of them as they show up at the park and learn about Chapman's death."

I decided to go along, since I didn't know what else to do with myself. I felt like sleeping, but I couldn't take a chance on going near the scoreboard in the daytime. It would be too easy to get caught by O'Hara.

We were almost to the Polo Grounds when I noticed how bad Runyon looked. "What time did you get up?" I asked.

Runyon gave me a sad smile. "I haven't been to bed. When a big story breaks, a reporter works straight through." He interrupted himself long enough to yawn, which caused me to show off my tonsils as well. "The hardest part was meeting the train that brought Chapman's widow from Cleveland. There was no way to let her know that Ray had died until she arrived."

"Did you have to tell her?"

"No, thank God. Speaker handled that." We both were quiet, imagining what it was like to tell a woman that her husband was dead.

When we got to the Polo Grounds, Runyon handed me a thermos from the backseat of his car and sent me down the street to have it filled with coffee. By the time I returned, the first few fans were arriving. No one could believe that Ray Chapman was gone. Instead of leaving when they learned that the game had been canceled, folks stood around, passing the news to the next bunch to arrive.

Eventually, talk turned to the pennant race. Everyone agreed that the Indians were finished. Even if they could overcome their heartache, they couldn't win without Chappie. A backup infielder named Harry Lunte would take over at shortstop. He wasn't in Ray's class as a fielder, and his hitting was pathetic.

The biggest arguments were between Yankee fans who thought that Carl Mays was washed up and would drag the team down with him, and those who thought that the path to the pennant was wide open. I didn't say anything, but the image of Mays weeping in the showers was in my head.

Black Sox and
Chocolate Sauce

By lunchtime, newsboys were on the street hawking an EXTRA edition of the *American*, its headline trumpeting "Chapman Dead." I took a copy and wandered the streets, looking for a peaceful place to read and think. I ended up on Coogan's Bluff, a kind of park above the Polo Grounds where bugs had gotten a free peek at the games for years. I sat with my back against a tree and read articles on Chappie until I was too sad to read about him anymore.

I tried to distract myself with a story on the Giants' upcoming series with the Phillies, but I couldn't concentrate. I know it sounds selfish, but all I could think of was my own future.

Ray Chapman was the first man to die playing major-league baseball, but how many others had seen their careers end in a split second because of an injury?

Supposing I was good enough, and lucky enough, to make it to the big time. What if I broke a leg and couldn't run the bases? Or got poked in the eye and couldn't spot the spin on a curve ball? With no schooling to fall back on, I could end up a bum like my old man.

No matter what job I had, I knew I wanted to travel. New York City was great, but I couldn't see a train without feeling the urge to climb on board and set off for parts unknown. What job other than baseball player would pay me to travel the country?

Then I thought of Damon Runyon. He went everywhere the Yankees went, and he didn't have to dodge killer fastballs. Maybe I should finish school. Then if things didn't pan out on the diamond, I could become a sportswriter.

I smiled, thinking how pleased John McGraw would be if I asked to return to Anson Academy. Then a terrible thought made me sit up, heart pounding. What if John McGraw, or Babe Ruth, or even Damon Runyon thought I was chickening out because of what happened to Ray Chapman? I couldn't stand it if any of those guys thought I was a coward. That got me to wondering if maybe I was a coward. How could I convince myself and everyone else that I wasn't being scared back to school?

The next day it seemed that no one wanted to be at the Polo Grounds. Fewer than two thousand bugs showed up, and they didn't know how to act. Babe Ruth hit a ball clear out of the stadium in batting practice. The bugs shot to their feet, then sat down, choking off their cheer as if enjoying themselves might be disrespectful.

The Indians were exhausted. In pregame warmups, I got a workout chasing bad throws. No one seemed to care where the ball went when they heaved it. I'm sure their minds were on the players not at the ballpark. Carl Mays was nowhere to be seen. Tris Speaker was on a train to Cleveland with Ray Chapman's body. The Indians would play the Yankees today and tomorrow, then go home for the funeral on Friday. Without their two best players, and with everyone else down in the dumps, they had no chance.

But the Yankees were listless, too. Cleveland starter Jim Bagby befuddled them, and the game went to the ninth inning with the Indians leading 3–2. The bugs began filing out of the ballpark. One mug who had sat along the left field line said, "Good for the Indians. They deserve to win after all they've been through." Nobody gave him an argument.

Then Duffy Lewis singled, bringing up Wally Pipp. The hard-hitting Pipp turned on a fastball and rifled it into the right field corner. The outfielder hustled, but the ball took a freakish hop off the wall and caromed toward the wide-open spaces of center field. While the Cleveland players chased the ball, Pipp raced around the base paths. When the throw home was wide of the mark, he slid across with an inside-the-park home run. Just like that, the Yankees had won the game. The few remaining bugs forgot that they were depressed and cheered long and loud. The Indians slunk off the field, heads low.

Cleveland won the final game of the series, this time holding a 3–2 lead. Babe Ruth hit his forty-third homer of the season, and no one seemed to notice. When the game ended, the Yankees trooped over to the visiting dugout and shook hands with the Cleveland players, sending them off on their sad journey to Ohio to bury a teammate.

Once the Indians left town, Carl Mays returned. I watched him out of the corner of my eye to see if he was acting different. Mays ran laps, threw a few pitches, and practiced bunting—all without a smile or a good word for anyone. He hadn't changed a bit.

Carl pitched against the Tigers on Monday. Ty Cobb was quoted in the papers saying that if a pitch came near him, there would be a fight. Mays kept the ball away from Cobb and everyone else. He pitched poorly, and the Tigers hit the ball hard, yet somehow they managed to shoot themselves in the foot over and over again.

Cobb had three hits, but was caught stealing twice. The Tigers hit into three double plays, all on vicious shots hit right at the nimble Yankee infielders. The Yankees slugged three home runs, including one by Ruth, and took the game by a score of 10–0.

Babe invited me to go for an ice cream after the game. Early in the season, Babe could walk the city streets without being recognized. Now, New Yorkers had seen his face plastered all over the newspapers for months. By the time we reached Sonny's Sodas and Sundaes, a mob of at least twenty kids was following us.

"Babe, welcome. Come in." A man with a thick mop of white hair greeted us at the door.

"This is . . . ," Babe introduced me.

I stuck out my hand. "Hank Cobb."

"I'm Sonny. Babe's good with faces, not names."

A chrome-trimmed counter lined with chrome stools with bright red, cushiony seats ran the length of the building. Lamps with colorful glass shades hung from the ceiling. If the lamps had been lit, I'd have needed George Burns's long-billed baseball cap to keep from being blinded by the reflected light in a mirror that covered one wall. But the lamps were dark, and the place as gloomy as a poolroom.

The crowd of kids tried to troop in behind us, but Sonny blocked the door. "Beat it. Paying customers only," he said, waving his arms.

"Ah, give the kids an ice-cream cone," Babe said. "You don't mind eating outside, do you, boys?"

The boys let out a roar. Sonny sighed and opened the freezer compartment closest to the door. He motioned me behind the counter and handed me one of those doohickeys you use to scoop ice cream. "You serve them, Hank. That sweet crap makes me sick." Man, was he in the wrong business.

I spent the next ten minutes scooping vanilla ice cream into sugar cones and passing them to the boys outside the door. When everyone was served, one of the older boys yelled, "Three cheers for Babe Ruth!" and the others gave a hip-hip-hooray.

Sonny returned to the door and said, "Now, go away. My regulars can't get near the place with you hooligans blocking the sidewalk." With one last cheer, the boys moved on.

"Kids. They're the worst part of this business," Sonny complained. "No offense to you, Hank."

I sat on a stool next to the Babe and looked around. Usually, an ice-cream parlor would be full of mothers and kids. Sonny's place was different. The stools were taken up by cigar-smoking men, reading the racing form. There was a tall curved glass like you would use to serve a milk shake or ice-cream soda in front of each customer. But even through the haze of smoke that filled the place, I smelled booze.

Sonny opened a metal compartment designed to hold a gallon of ice cream. He pulled out a bottle of hooch and, being careful to keep it below the counter, poured a healthy belt into a parfait glass. He passed it to Babe, who took a swig. Babe's eyes met mine as he wiped his mouth on his sleeve. "You didn't make yourself anything, Kid."

Sonny grunted, "On the house. You earned it."

That was an invitation I didn't need to hear twice. I squeezed past Sonny and took a long, metal dish from a shelf. I had left the scoop soaking in a pan of water. I pulled it out and started yanking up metal hatches. Under each was a different type of booze.

Sonny pointed toward the door. The last three compartments held ice cream. I loaded up with a scoop each of chocolate, vanilla, and strawberry, then began reading the labels on the syrup pumps. "They're dummies, except for the chocolate sauce," Sonny mumbled. That was my favorite, anyway. I pumped until my ice cream was floating. Then I grabbed a spoon and rejoined the Babe.

"Did you beat those Tigers today?" asked one of the cigar smokers.

"Ten to nothing," Babe said.

"Mays pitched good?"

"Good enough." Babe shrugged.

The man pulled the cigar from his mouth, exposing the bite marks on its slimy end. It was enough to put me off my sundae for a minute. "What's the dope on the White Sox? Is it true that they threw the World Series?" he asked.

Babe banged his glass on the counter. "No way. I've known some of those boys for years. They want to win as bad as anybody."

"Yeah? Well, I hear the fix was in," he insisted, clamping the cigar between his teeth. "How else could the Reds beat 'em? That bunch of humpties couldn't hit my fastball."

My head was spinning. Was that why John McGraw wouldn't talk about the World Series? I remembered how he had refused to introduce me to Shoeless Joe Jackson in spring training.

Babe stood up and glowered. "If you don't want to eat that cigar, you'd better keep your opinions to yourself." He tossed a five-dollar bill on the counter, grabbed my arm, splattering chocolate sauce down my shirt front, and hustled us out the door.

Babe dragged me down the street. When we reached

the corner, I managed to pull my arm free. "What's wrong, Babe?"

He blinked as if he hadn't realized he had hold of me. "Sorry, Kid. Talk like that makes me sick. How many people will pay to see us play if they think the games are fixed?"

"That guy is nuts," I said, wanting to believe it. "Why would the White Sox lose on purpose?"

Babe sighed. "If they did, and I don't believe it for a minute, it's because of that cheapskate who owns the team."

"Charles Comiskey?"

"That's the one. You want to know how stingy he is? Last year he started charging the players to wash their uniforms."

"You're kidding."

"It's true. So Cicotte talked the others into playing dirty. They wore the same outfit, game after game, for two weeks. Sportswriters didn't know what was going on. Started calling them the Black Sox."

"Don't they make good money? I've been around the big leagues over a year now, and every player I've met has cash in his pocket."

"They're not starving, Kid. But they're not getting what they deserve, either. Comiskey made a fortune last year, and he's got the smallest payroll in baseball." Babe lowered his voice. "You saw what happened to Chappie. No one knows how long they'll be able to play this game. You've got to make as much money as you can those few years when you're at your peak. Most of us aren't good at anything but playing baseball."

Babe said more, but I missed it. He had started me thinking about school again. I wanted to be a ballplayer, but I wanted to have something else I could count on, a way to earn a living when my playing days were over. When John McGraw returned, I was going to ask to go back to school. Between now and then I had to find a way to prove to myself and everyone else that I wasn't leaving out of fear.

Losing Control

M y chance came after Carl Mays's next start, the day before John McGraw was due in New York. The White Sox had clobbered the Yankees the previous day, 16–4. I wondered if the cigar chomper thought they were trying to lose that game. The loss left the Yankees four games out of first place, trailing both Cleveland and Chicago. Mays took the mound with the team in desperate need of a win.

Mays did well against left-handed hitters, but the righties were digging in and teeing off. It only took a couple of innings for them to realize that Carl Mays wasn't the fearless pitcher who used to terrorize them. He threw pitch after pitch over the heart of the plate. The White Sox hitters bashed them to all corners of the park.

Ping Bodie trotted off the field with the Babe, after running down two long drives in left center field. "I'm too tired to hit," he complained. Luckily, Babe wasn't. He smacked three doubles, and the Yankees won 6–5.

Huggins tried to talk to Mays after the game, but Carl draped a towel over his head and ignored him. He stayed in the dugout until his teammates had showered and left. I was waiting for him, still in uniform. When Mays realized he wasn't alone, he snapped, "What do you want?"

I took a deep breath. "I think we can help each other."

Mays snorted. "Things are bad, but not so bad that I need a punk kid to help me."

"Well, I need you," I admitted.

I expected Mays to run me off. His eyes flashed with anger, then calmed. "I appreciate that you never told anyone about the shower. I thought you'd go straight to Runyon. I didn't want to read in the papers that I was soft-hearted." So he had seen me that day. "Maybe I owe you a favor," Mays said.

"I want to bat against you."

"What, kick me when I'm down? I may be having trouble with my control, but if I couldn't strike you out, I'd quit the game."

"It's something I need to do."

"Why?" Mays asked.

"I want to go back to school. But I want to make sure I'm not leaving because I'm afraid."

Mays snorted. "You belong in school. Besides, it's common sense to be scared."

This would be the hard part. "I think you're afraid, too. You don't pitch the way you used to."

Mays looked like he might take a swing at me, then

got control of himself. "I'm just a little wild lately." He could see I didn't believe him. "Even if I was scared, how would pitching to you help me?"

"I'm right-handed. You could practice brushing me back. When you see nothing bad happens, maybe you'll be able to do it in a game again."

"What if I plug you? I can see the headlines. 'Crazed Pitcher Beans Scrawny Kid.'"

I ignored the insult. "I'm quick. I can get out of the way of anything you throw." Mays still seemed reluctant, so I added, "Besides, I think I can hit you."

That did the trick. "Be here at ten tomorrow. And be ready to duck." He pulled his jersey over his head and trudged to the showers.

Last Licks

I gave up trying to sleep long before daybreak. Every time I shut my eyes, I saw Carl Mays staring down at me from the pitcher's mound. Would I be so afraid that I couldn't hold the bat still? I left the ballpark and walked the streets until I saw the lights go on in a place called Joe's. The old man once told me that a condemned man could order anything he wanted as a last meal. I figured I was entitled to some flapjacks.

When the waitress served me, I took my stack apart, coated each hot cake with butter and strawberry jam, then put the pile together again. My stomach must be dumber than the rest of me, because food was the only thing it was worried about. In five minutes, my plate was bare except for a red stain left by the jam. A quick scrape with my pinkie, and that dish looked clean enough to use again.

It was still way before ten when I got to the Polo Grounds, so I went looking for O'Hara. "How are you with a paintbrush?" he asked. "The outfield fence could use a touch-up."

I said, "Good enough to get by," which earned me a perch on a ladder. O'Hara held it steady while I slopped paint on the wooden boards. We started at the left field foul pole, and I was almost to the billboard for Ajax Flypaper when I heard the unmistakable sound of a baseball hitting a mitt.

I looked over my shoulder. Carl Mays was warming up on the mound. I sprayed a brushload of paint on O'Hara instead of the wall. "I've got to go," I said and climbed down, dripping paint onto our hands as I passed O'Hara the brush. I couldn't tell you what he said to me.

Scared as I was, I studied Mays's delivery on my way to the dugout. His pitching arm nearly dragged on the ground, then sprang toward home plate like a rattlesnake striking its prey.

I stopped near third base, and Mays quit throwing to the catcher to stare at me. "Get in uniform. I'm almost ready," he said. He made a circular motion with his right hand, signaling the catcher that he was going to throw a curve ball. I wished he would be that obvious when I was up at bat.

I didn't have time to scrub the paint off my hands, but I made sure there was nothing wet to stain my uniform. I pulled on the Yankees jersey, hoping Mays would see me as a teammate more than an opponent. Not that he had ever shown much regard for either one.

My stomach was joining the rest of my body in panic. Those flapjacks sat like a lead ball, weighing me down when I needed to be quickest. I pulled the lighter of my two bats out of the locker and did a few stretches, one hand gripping each end. My muscles felt tight, as if the slightest jerk might tear them loose from my bones.

My spirits lifted. If I hurt myself hacking at the first pitch, I could beg off. Mays wouldn't expect me to face him injured. But if I pulled that stunt, I'd have the answer to my question. I would know that I lacked the nerve to be a professional baseballer. If I wanted to accept that I was a coward, I didn't have to go to bat at all.

I looked up to see the catcher staring at me from the doorway to the dugout. It wasn't the Yankees' regular backstop, Muddy Ruel. Face hidden by the catcher's mask, he jerked his thumb in the air. I followed him to the diamond, feeling a little like one of those poor souls who follows Death to a graveyard in a scary story.

Mays was pacing back and forth, so I took my stance. The catcher got into his crouch, still without saying a word. I sucked in a lungful of air and gripped the bat all the way down on the knob, just like the Babe.

Mays eyeballed the catcher with a steely concentration that turned my knees to jelly. His arms flew over his head. He rocked, then plunged his right arm toward the ground. Suddenly, the ball raced at me. I leaned away, nearly dropping my bat. The pitch crossed the outside corner of the plate.

"Strike," Mays barked. "A little skittish, aren't you?" Twice more he delivered, and twice more I flinched, only to see the ball sail through the strike zone. With each pitch, my hands inched farther up the bat handle. Free swinging was great if you had a pitcher's number. Fighting for my life, I was falling back on every trick John McGraw had ever taught me.

I finally got the bat off my shoulder, but missed so badly that Mays snorted in disgust. My face burned with shame, but there was anger, too. I loved baseball, and I wasn't going to let Carl Mays or anyone else run me off. I dug in, determined to hold my ground.

Mays must have wheeled his arm, rocked, and dipped, but I never saw him. I focused on the right edge of the pitching rubber, the spot where he always released the ball. The pitch shot homeward, but this time I was on it from the instant it left his hand. I slapped at it and fouled it behind first base. That shred of contact made batting against Carl Mays seem possible.

Mays gave a nasty laugh and called, "Watch yourself, Hank," trying to scare me. I was already too shaky to feel any worse. I stayed focused on that corner of the pitching rubber. The ball sped homeward, but I could see it would be too high. The catcher leaped from his crouch to grab it.

"Ball," I announced and scraped up some dust with my cleats to see if I could get a reaction from that mummy behind the plate. The catcher didn't say anything, but his throw back to the pitcher zipped between the bill of my cap and my nose.

The next pitch came right at me. I jumped back, but the extra second I had hesitated, determined not to look like a sissy, nearly did me in. The ball brushed my baggy jersey and struck the knob of the bat.

It's going to sound strange, but coming that close to getting creamed and escaping built my confidence. For the first time, I truly believed that no matter what pitch Carl Mays threw, my reflexes were quick enough to avoid it. I'd spent my life ducking everything from my old man's blows to the grasp of railroad cops. The thing I was best at was getting out of danger. I might never know why Ray Chapman had frozen in front of a fastball on that fatal day, but I knew now that it had nothing to do with me.

The pitch did something for Carl Mays, too. He had come inside, and I had done what a batter was supposed to do, what they had always done before August 16. I won't say it was fun standing up there. It took all my concentration and nerve. By the time Mays yelled, "That's enough," I was exhausted.

I hadn't hit anything but a few weak grounders and a couple of pop-ups, but I felt like I had won the World Series. The catcher slapped me on the rear end with his mitt and said, "You've got guts, Hank."

My jaw dropped. There was no mistaking John McGraw's voice. He pulled off his mask and grinned at me for the first time since he thought I had jinxed the Yankees. Mays joined us, shaking hands with McGraw. "Does he have the makings of a ballplayer?" McGraw asked.

"He has a better head on his shoulders than Ruth," Mays said, turning toward the dugout. "I've got a train to catch."

John McGraw looped an arm over my shoulder. "Carl's not much for praise. You've got potential, Hank. You kept your head under pressure." He gave me a half smile. "I noticed your hands sliding up the bat after those first couple of pitches."

"When I was overmatched, all the things you taught me came flooding back." I looked at the ground.

McGraw squeezed my shoulder. "I need a shower. I'm too old for squatting behind the plate, especially with a batter who kicks dirt in your face." I could feel the color in my cheeks.

"Come to dinner tonight, Hank. I think the missus is baking again."

"I'll be there," I promised.

Graham Court Verdict

T he spread couldn't compare with Colonel Ruppert's, just meat loaf, cabbage, and baked potatoes, but there was nowhere I would rather have had dinner. John McGraw had come to the Polo Grounds in the middle of a pennant race, just to make sure I was safe. No matter how gruff he acted at times, I knew now that he cared.

Mrs. McGraw cleared the table, leaving us to loosen our belts and get ready for the apple pie and coffee that would follow. McGraw was all smiles. The Giants were playing his type of baseball, and they were in the thick of the pennant race. He reached under his chair and held up the late edition of the *World*. Half the back page was a closeup of McGraw studying his lineup card. The headline read, "McGraw—Strategy Tops Power."

"The writers have decided that I know what I'm doing after all, Hank."

"Nobody knows baseball better than you," I said and meant it.

McGraw let out a gust of air. "Baseball, yes, but I'm not always so good with people. I rushed you, Hank. Instead of giving you time to figure things out for yourself, I tried to force you to see things my way. If I could erase that day I pitched to you, I would."

"I was out of line, too," I admitted. "When I escaped from the old man, I promised myself that no one would ever push me around again. I know now that you meant well."

McGraw stuck his hand across the table. I squeezed it, trying to match his iron grip. We were each waiting for the other to release when Mrs. McGraw came in carrying the dessert and coffee. We let go, and she set the tray between us.

"Who saved room for apple pie?" she asked.

"I've got one more thing to say before we dig in," I announced. "I want to finish school."

Mrs. McGraw beamed. "Why the change of heart?" John McGraw wondered.

"When Ray Chapman went down, I saw how fast things can change in life. A guy has to develop all his talents if he wants to be prepared for whatever comes along."

"Will you go back to Anson Academy?" Mrs. McGraw asked.

"No, I'd like to try the local school, live here, and keep my job at the Polo Grounds . . . if that's all right."

"Nothing could please me more . . . except winning another pennant," McGraw said. That made us all laugh.

An hour later, I lay on my bed staring at the ceiling, the sweetness of the apple pie making me put off cleaning my teeth. It might be years before I was ready, but I knew that someday I'd get a shot at the big leagues. I'd step to the plate, the stands full of screaming bugs and a tough pitcher on the mound. I'd be scared, but I wouldn't back down. If I could face Carl Mays, I could do anything.

Author's
Note

N either the Giants nor the Yankees made it to the World Series in 1920. To the wonder of all, the Cleveland Indians recovered from the tragic death of Ray Chapman to win the title, beating the Brooklyn Robins in seven games. Joe Sewell, a five-foot-seven shortstop in his first year as a professional, led the charge. Joe batted .329 and manned the difficult position like a veteran. Sewell went on to play in over seven thousand games as an Indian and Yankee. He is remembered today as the most difficult player to strike out in baseball history, fanning as few as four times in a season, and only 114 times in his long career.

Babe Ruth ended the season with fifty-four home runs. The St. Louis Browns were the only *team* in the league to approach Ruth's total, hitting fifty round-trippers. Babe's sensational career in New York had just begun. He went on to lead the Yankees to the first four of their record twenty-six championships. His popularity generated the money to build Yankee Stadium, the storied facility that housed baseball's most successful team, from opening day in 1923 until the end of the 2008 season.

I tried to capture the good and bad aspects of Babe's personality. He was soft-hearted, crude, expansive, and reckless—sometimes all in the same day. Ruth was a frequent visitor to my hometown of Tuxedo, New York, attracted by its hunting and fishing opportunities. I grew up hearing stories of his kindness and generosity. As a young man, my father earned extra money working as a chauffeur on weekends. He once drove Babe Ruth to a funeral and never forgot how Babe cried openly at the church service and in the cemetery.

The incident with the Locomobile is made up, but Babe's career was dotted with traffic accidents, and he had at least two during the 1920 season. It is a fact that Babe called for a baseball bat to repair his injured knee after an ill-advised attempt to steal second base.

Drop the Dip was the most thrilling roller coaster of its day, and the first to feature a safety bar. It opened at Coney Island in 1907, burned to the ground during its first season, and was rebuilt. It ran until the mid-1930s, renamed Trip to the Moon near the end of its existence.

John McGraw was always searching for a competitive edge. Keeping the Mexican wildcat, Bill Pennant, as a mascot was one of many attempts he made to ensure that Lady Luck would be on the side of the New York Giants.

Yankee owner Jacob Ruppert did raise exotic animals on his Garrison estate, but Bill Pennant's adoption is fictional. All mention of the feisty wildcat stopped near the end of spring training, and I have not been able to learn what happened to him. I like to imagine that he escaped into the wilderness and lived a long and happy life free from people and cages.